# The Legendary Hero

*Welcome to a book about fantasy, magic and swords*

# Part 1 - The Three Princesses

By Eric Thompson

*Introduction*

Once upon a time in a land far away, there lived a king, queen, and four princesses. The kingdom was in a state of happiness and joy.

It feels so good to be here said Isabelle.

Me too, said Gloria.

And us, said Summer and Violet.

We live in a great castle. Don't we sisters?

Yes Isabelle.

I don't see that something bad is going to happen.

We don't either, said the king and queen. We live in a land where everything is secure and so many wonders. Suddenly the lights dimmed. An evil witch appeared out of nowhere.

The soldiers looked on with surprise. Their spears and swords were armed.

The King and Queen looked at her in anger.

The king said, Who are You?

I'm Belinda the evil witch. This place is full of goodness. "You princesses have everything that I need. I will take your sister Isabelle and you will never see her again. Ha, Ha, Ha.". The soldiers said if you want to capture her you'll have to go through us!! You soldiers are no match for my powers.

Charge!! When the soldiers tried to rescue the kidnapped princess, Belinda pushed them away with her power.

SHAY!!

She tied up Isabelle with cords.

Mela!!

Let me Go!! Said Isabelle.

Let our Sister Go!!

Gloria lunged for the wand but Belinda stepped out of her way.

It was no use. Her other sisters could not stop the kidnapping. Belinda was much too powerful to be overcome.

We will get our sister back! Said Summer.

Oh I'd like to see you try princess! said Belinda.

The three princesses were alone.

Summer said, "My goodness, that evil witch is powerful."

The three sisters looked on in horror to see their sister being taken away.

"How will we ever get her back?"

Those that lived in the kingdom felt that all was lost as despair took over. Was there not someone in the kingdom who could overcome the evil that was spreading throughout the land? Would the three princesses ever see their                              sister                              again?

# Chapter 1
# The Legendary Hero

The Legendary Hero was in his lab contemplating his sudden transformation from Spider-Man. He had everything. A lab that had a computer, threat detector, kitchen, a study room and most importantly a door that he could enter through a shed. He also had weapons of every kind in his possession. He remembered what Spider-Man told him. "You are the legendary Hero!" "I'm giving you the opportunity to become the most powerful hero in the world!" It was his destiny to become a superhero and make a difference in the world. While he was contemplating he heard a noise from the threat detector.

Computer!!

Yes Legendary Hero??

I hear something.

Threat detected!! Shall I play it for you?

Yes!!

Ok!!

Oh my goodness!! I see a Princess being captured!! Computer!! Track the location!!

The computer found where the threat was.

Shall I save this location for you?

Yes. Please!! So this is where it is. Somewhere far away. I wish I could go there and stop her but that wouldn't mean anything. Is it even necessary for princesses to be heroes and save their sister? Usually the men are the heroes so maybe instead the princesses can be trained to stop the evil that's around them. So I basically need to find two warriors who can train the princesses. But who? Perhaps I can find a swordsman, a wizard and a keeper of weapons. But where to find them. I don't know.

Perhaps I'll be able to find them once the computer narrows them down since it sees and hears everything through a satellite. Computer?

Yes Legendary Hero?

Keep your eye out for 3 people. One who wants to be a swordsman, another who wants to be a wizard and a guy named Fred.

Yes.

So he waited and waited. After a long time the computer found three people.

Legendary Hero!! I've found three people!!

Excellent!! Where are they located?

Pinpointing locations. One at Eric's Domain, the second at Aubreyville and the third in this city.

Excellent!! I should go to these locations. Before I go I should talk to Spider-Man about my discoveries. Computer!!

Yes?

Call Spider-Man.

Calling Spider-Man…..

Hello? This is your friendly neighborhood Spider-Man.

Hey spidey.

Legendary Hero!! What's up?

I thought you should know that I found two warriors.

Two warriors?

Yep.

What for?

Well I found out that a princess was captured by an evil witch named Belinda.

Really?

Yes.

So you're finding two warriors for what exactly?

The princess has three younger sisters.

Oh I understand now. You're trying to help them rescue their sister.

That's right.

That's awesome. Good luck to you.

Thank you Spider-Man. Oh!! I forgot to tell you about the evil witch.

What about her?

I'm thinking I should appear to the princess and see her.

Seriously?? You want to rescue her all by yourself?

No. That's not what I mean. I want to give her hope and let her know that her sisters are coming to rescue her.

I understand. That's ok. It could be dangerous.

I understand Spider-Man. I won't be captured. Thanks again.

You're welcome.

Bye.

Wow!! I just got approval to go to the evil witches' lair. Computer!!

Yes??

Take me to the Evil witches lair.

I've found it. Beginning transportation.

He was sent to the evil witches' lair.


The legendary Hero stealthily entered into the evil witches' lair.

He saw Isabel tied up.

He looked at Belinda with fury in his eyes.

BELINDA!! You let Isabelle Go!!

Belinda looked over with an evil glint in her eyes. "Well, if it isn't the legendary hero. Isabel will never be free. Ha, Ha, Ha."

Isabelle screamed, "Let me out! I want to be with my sisters."

"You will never get out."

Isabelle again screamed, "Help! Help!"

The legendary hero looked at Isabelle. "Don't worry Isabelle." I will get you out."

"How?" asked Isabelle.

"I will be back and will be able to free you. Your sisters will come."

"They will?"

"Yes. I also have two warriors that will help them."

"You do?"

"Yes. Have hope."

"Thank you, sir," responded Isabelle. "Who are you?"

I'm the Legendary Hero.

Thank you for coming by.

It was my pleasure. This isn't over yet Belinda!!

On the contrary, it's only just begun. And soon I'll build my evil army. Ha ha ha……

Belinda smiled while the Legendary Hero left.

So nice to have Isabelle hostage.

You have NO Right to hold me here!!

And why not princess? Because my sisters need me. I'm the one who is the wisest. Without me they can't learn their skills. I am the oldest and I deserve to help them.

I like having you here Isabelle.

Well I don't!!

You're not going anywhere!


Well! That went well, said the Legendary Hero as he left Belinda's lair. Isabelle seemed upset to be captive. He headed back to Eric's Domain.

He spoke a command. Where are the warriors located?

The radar pinpointed where the warriors were.

This is great. I've found where they are. It is time to locate them and find the princesses.

The Legendary Hero thought about the locations and said "Porifay". He appeared in the city.

It is time to find the man who wants to be a wizard. Looks like my phone should keep track of where he is.

# Chapter 2 Elphias

While the Legendary Hero was searching on his phone for the man he needed to find, the man was in his home upstairs reading a book.

"My! Oh my! What a day," he said.

He wanted to learn about magic. He began his study by reading a book on magic titled, *A Guide to Survival by the Legendary Hero.*

"Hmmmm… This legendary hero exists? Ok."

He learned that there is no reason to be afraid of magic. Magic has power beyond anything you have imagined, but it also has limits. Magic is protective. Magic is performed by wizards. To consider becoming a wizard you must learn the steps which are: be brave, don't underestimate your enemies, show your powers, always trust the legendary hero, and be strong.

"Wow! This book on magic is very interesting. I wish I were a wizard."

To perform magic a wizard must have a wand.

"Where can I go to get a wand? That's a good question."

Suddenly there was a knock on the door.

My goodness!! Who could that be at this time of day? The police? The paparazzi? Pizza guy? I should check it out.

He looked through the hole and saw it was a man dressed in a black cape with a black mask standing there.

Hello? Can I help you sir?

Why yes. I'm the Legendary Hero. Can I come in?

Um,                                                                                         sure.

# Chapter 3
## The Legendary Hero Meets Elphias

Who are you?"

"I am the legendary hero."

What's your name?

I'm Elphias. "Where did you come from?"

"I came from my home."

"Where is your home?"

"I have a home in the light of Eric Thompson's domain, which is in the land of Mystika. I have a friend there named Spider-Man.

Spider-Man? The Spider-Man?

Yes. That's right.

"How did you become a wizard?"

"That's a very good question. A long time ago I was chosen to become the most powerful hero the world has ever known by my master Spiderman.

"Are you serious? How come he was your mentor?"

"I looked up to him and he made everything possible for me. He told me that I could also become the most powerful superhero in the world.

"Can you tell me how you came to be who you are?"

"Yes.                           Of                           course!"

# Chapter 4
# The Legendary Hero's Story

The legendary hero looked at the man. "Well, it all started like this. I was secretly reading books and had no friends."

"What was it like to be alone?"

"I didn't like it much. But little did I know that I was being watched. So, I went around just doing nothing and being sad. While I was alone, there was a superhero named Spider Man. He saw me and said to himself, *"This boy is very lonely. Maybe I should find friends for him."* Spiderman went to see the superheroes and held a meeting with them. They asked, "What has become of this boy? Is he the one that will bring peace and justice to this world?"

Spiderman stepped forward.

"My friends. Settle down. There is no need to fear. I know he is the chosen one because he is young and he will have amazing powers just like us except his powers will last forever."

"Do you think that's possible Spider-Man?"

"Yes. All we have to do is visit with him and then we will give him what he deserves. He will have us as friends and he will also receive a machine that will take him anywhere he wants to go by saying a command for the hero he wants to become. He just has to say it."

"Your plan is amazing Spiderman. Let's go see him."

# Chapter 5
# Demetrius's Discovery and Destiny

Demetrius was sitting at his desk at home. His friends from High School were gone and he was all alone. He was sad. He bowed down in shame.

"Man, I wish I had friends."

Suddenly there was a knock at his door.

Well well. I wonder who that could be.

"Surprise!

Whoa! Who are you guys?"

Spiderman steps forward. "We are the superheroes.

We want to be your friends."

"Thank you.

What is your name?"

"Demetrius."

"That's a good name. Demetrius, you are

privileged to become something more."

"What's that?"

"Destiny Demetrius. Destiny. You will have the opportunity of a lifetime to become the most powerful hero in the world."

"How?"

"I am going to give you my powers and everyone else will too."

"How?"

"I have a machine here. Do you want it?"

"Sure."

"This is a threat detector that can find anything that doesn't seem right, even a distress signal. This is the computer that will locate wherever the disturbance is coming from. To become a superhero you just have to say the name and you'll become it. You also have a wand that can take you anywhere you desire to go. All you have to do is say "Porifay " and you'll be able to go wherever you want. Although I must warn you. It only works for one person at a time. To send a whole group you have to request it from the computer and it will transport them wherever they want to go. One last thing to remember about the computer. You can create virtual commands where you can practice fighting enemies which is pretty cool."

"Thank you, Spiderman."

"You're welcome Demetrius"

One last thing for you to learn.

What's that?

You get to learn how to use a lightsaber.

That's interesting. How do I use a lightsaber?

Spider-Man asked one of the superheroes to demonstrate.

I'm a guardian of peace.

He pressed the button.

Do you see that?

I do.

You can use this to block and attack. Push with your hand. This is power that you can use. Use it to push enemies away. Now you try.

Demetrius held the lightsaber. It felt strong in his hands.

With this kind of power I can make a difference and defend good from evil.

Well said Demetrius.

Thank you superheroes.

# Chapter 6
# Legendary Hero Trains Elphias

The man scratches his ear. "Wow, legendary hero. That is a great story. "How did you do it?'

"Well, like I said before," the legendary hero responded. "I used my machine and the enemies appeared right there."

"What else can you tell me about the princesses?"

"Well, there is much to know about them. A long time ago they were together, happy, and everything was peaceful."

"How did you know that one was captured?"

"When I came home, I noticed that a light was blinking and I heard a beeping noise. I thought, *what is that noise?* My eyes drifted toward my computer. It told me I had a message. The message was that the witch had captured the princesses' oldest sister. This is the reason I came to see you, Elphias. The three princesses will be the heroes to rescue their sister, not the men."

"Why not the men?"

"Because the princesses want to be like and follow their oldest sister but they can't because she is captured. They don't have magic powers either."

"How are they going to gain those powers?"

"They are very young, Elphias. They are also brave. They will do as we say because without our help they will not be able to stop the evil witch. I even talked to the evil witch."

"You? How did you do that?"

"After I received the message about Isabelle's capture, I went to the land where the evil witch lived and verified that the princess was a captive. I went inside where she was being held, found Belinda and told her to let Isabelle go."

That's crazy. Did she let her go?

No. I just listened after I left. Isabelle seemed pretty upset.

So how do I learn to be a wizard?"

"Well that's simple really. All you have to do is get a wand."

First off before we go, what is your name?

Elphias.

Elphias. That's a nice name.

Thank you. "So. Where can I get a wand?"

"Follow me into the city and I'll show you."

"There are so many stores here. Which one is it?"

"We are going to a place called Wands Extraordinaire."

"Ah! Here we are."

They opened the shop door. Someone shouted, "Thief!! Stop him."

"Elphias!! Wait. Stop right there. Thief!!" "**DEZMO!**"

The thief stopped instantly. "Aaahhh!! Don't hurt me…"

The legendary hero asks, "Now, why would you steal a wand? Tell Me!!! Now!!!"

"Ok. Ok. I want to make people disappear."

"Give me that wand. Get out of here and don't steal. If I ever see you do it again, you are toast."

**Strasinko!**

The attack sent him reeling out the door into a bush.

Well that's that.

"Thank you. You saved the day."

"All in a day's work. It was my pleasure!!"

"Tell me… What wand do you have for this man Elphias?"

The storekeeper holds up a wand. "Let me see… This wand is a little small and breaks objects." The storekeeper picks up another wand. "Now this one... Hmm… It is lengthy, very thick and the tip lightens up.

Let me test this one, said Demetrius. Elphias. Give it a flick.

He flicked it.

It's perfect. We'll take this one said Demetrius. That will be five dollars."

"I'll pay for him."

"Thanks again."

The legendary hero and Elphias left the store.

"Wow! How did you do that? That was amazing."

"Well, like I said in my story, I am a hero."

"Now what do we do? Asked Elphias.

"We go to a field. Hold onto my hand."

"Ok."

Whish… They landed in the field.

"How did you do that?"

"Magic."

# Chapter 7
# Elphias Trains

They land in the midst of the trees.

"Elphias?"

"Yes?"

"I am going to teach you how to use your wand. Follow along with me. Point your wand and say strasinko, strasinko. Try it on me."

Elphias pointed his wand and issued the command. "**STRASINKO!**"

"Well done Elphias. You knocked me down. Now, the next spell that will stun your opponent is dezmo."

"**DEZMO!**"

"Good, you stunned me. Well Done! To light your wand, say ignite."

"**IGNITE!**"

"Good job Elphias, you are ready to become a wizard. That spell you just cast lights up your wand. Awesome. Now you are ready."

"What do we do now?"

I'm going to pay a visit to Frederick of Galvestein.

Keep practicing and we'll meet up soon.

# Chapter 8
## Demetrius Locates Frederick

I've been successful finding Elphias and now I need to find Frederick. I wonder if there's a way to fix the computer and the transportation. I recall my master Braille mentioning that he almost got captured by villains who came through a portal at the same location that he was at. If I tried to fix it I would have the same fate. Perhaps after Malcolm's defeat I should try again. I understand that it's dangerous but I think it's possible. Perhaps an update needs to be in order. I can look into this later. I need to find Frederick. Computer?

Yes?

Find Frederick.

Locating......

He's in Galvestein. Do you want me to transport you?

No thanks.

Demetrius pointed his wand and said "Porifay to Galvestein!"

I've made it safely to Galvestein. Now to find Frederick.

# Chapter 9
# Frederick of Galvestein

Living in the land of Mystika was very interesting. It was purple and a man had a purple house. The man was walking around his home reading about skills and survival. The title of the book he was reading was *Survival and What It Means to be a Fighter* by the legendary hero. It talks about fighting and protecting yourself.

He asked himself, *"What is survival?"*

In the book he found the definition. *Survival is the instinct of staying alive. Survival is the way to be victorious.*

Again, he wondered, *"What does it mean to be a fighter?"*

The book once again provided the answer. *"Fighting can keep enemies from succeeding."*

He wondered, *"How?"*

He kept reading and found the answer. *"Having courage and bravery. Courage is standing strong and proving justice to anyone that stands in the way. With practice you can be unstoppable."*

He thought. *"Wow. I am not a swordsman but it would be nice to become one. What can I do? I don't have a sword."*

He left his home and came to the city where he met someone.

"Hello. How are you?"

"I am doing well."

"Where are you going?"

"I am going to find a sword."

"Why do you need a sword?"

"Because I want to learn how to be a swordsman."

"Where did you learn about this?"

"I read a book titled *Survival and What It Means to be a Fighter* by the legendary hero."

"That's interesting. Have a good day."

He went home and back to his studies. He became deep in thought. *"So, it says here you can become a swordsman. But how? There's nothing I can do."*

Poof!

# Chapter 10
## The Legendary Hero Meets Frederick

The legendary hero came to the man's house and knocked on the door. Knock, knock, knock.

He said, "Hello. Who is it?"

"The legendary hero. Can I come in?"

"Yes. So, what brings you here?"

"I am the legendary hero and have come here to train you. There is much you need to learn. I am going to teach you how to be a swordsman. I am going to train you for a big opportunity."

"What is that?"

"You will become wise like me so you can show the princesses how to fight."

"Are you serious? They're fighting? I thought that only men would fight."

"Normally, they do, but this is more serious."

"What happened?"

"Well, an evil witch named Belinda captured the princesses' sister, Isabelle."

"How?"

"Belinda had evil magic that she used to wrap Isabelle in cords. Magic is one thing that should never be underestimated. Now, the first lesson, always mind your surroundings, second have a sword and shield to protect yourself, third hit an enemy and they'll poof in smoke. I guarantee that if you do these things you will become wise like me."

"Is there anything you want, legendary hero?"

"Yes."

"What?"

"I would like a drink of water." He gave the hero some water and he drank.

"So, you are Frederick of Galvestein?"

"Yes, I am. You know my name?"

"Yes."

"How do you know?"

"I just know because I needed to find someone who I could train and I looked on the computer.

That is very interesting legendary Hero.

So…..What will I learn today?"

"Today you will learn about a sword and how simple it is to use."

# Chapter 11
# Frederick Fights with a Sword

Frederick asked, "Me? Using a sword? I don't know how."

The legendary hero, holding his sword, said, "I'll show you. Here is my sword. Feel it. It is smooth on the surface. What do you see?"

"Trees."

"Anything else?"

"Nope."

"Ok. I will get you a sword. The legendary hero went back to his shop and found a sword and two shields. On his return, Frederick asked, "Do we have shields?"

"Yes."

"What do we need these for?"

"These are to protect us from enemies."

"Where can we find enemies?"

"Follow me."

Frederick followed the legendary hero back to his home. Upon entering, he noticed the machine. "Wow! That is a great machine. What does it do?"

The legendary hero issued a command, "COMPUTER! SEND US SOME ENEMIES." As soon as he said that, they were completely surrounded by enemies.

"Aaahhh!" yelled Frederick. There are too many of them."

"Watch and learn!!" The legendary hero swung his sword in angles and strokes and defeated every one.

"Whooah!" Frederick exclaimed. "They vanished in smoke."

"Right. Now Frederick, you will fight with your sword. Are you ready?

The legendary hero pressed the button on the machine again and the enemies reappeared. "You shall not prevail!" With those words of power Frederick fought with the sword just like the hero and he succeeded.

"Well done Frederick."

"Thank you, legendary hero."

"You are now ready to help the princesses defeat the evil witch, Belinda."

"But, there are three princesses?"

"Yes."

"Belinda has captured their oldest sister. Only you, the wizard Elphias, and I can help them on their quest to rescue their sister."

"Now, what do I do?"

"Just wait. Practice and practice with the sword like I showed you. Soon all three of us will have a meeting where we will prove justice to the evil that is spreading."

"When?"

"You will know when I return.

When will that be?

Very soon. I'll call you.

Sounds great.

He returned to Eric's Domain to check in with Spider-Man one more time.

# Chapter 12
## The Legendary Hero speaks with Spider-Man

It feels good to be back in Eric's Domain.

I've been able to find the warriors that I've needed and am ready to send them on their quest to find the princesses and train them. So now I'm calling Spider-Man one more time to report. Computer!!

Yes?

Call Spider-Man.

Calling Spider-Man…..

Hello. This is your friendly neighborhood Spider-Man.

Hey Spidey. It's the Legendary Hero again.

Hi. What's up?

I've completed everything I needed to do.

You found the warriors?

Yep.

You found the princesses?

Yep.

Looks like you have completed everything. All that remains is for you to find the princesses. Well done!!

Thank you Spider-Man. I shall see you again. Bye.

It is time for the warriors to go on their quest.

# Chapter 13
# Preparations


*Hmmm… These princesses would want anything to save their sister,* *thought* the legendary hero. *What should I do?* So, he contacted Fred, Frederick of Galvestein and Elphias and asked to meet with them.

They got together quickly. The legendary hero looked at the three of them. "We have come together for a reason."

"What is the reason?" Elphias asked.

"There are three princesses who want to save their sister Isabelle who was captured by the evil witch Belinda."

"Is this true?"

"Yes."

"What should we do?" asked Fred.

"Since I, the legendary hero. know the prophecy, I will tell you where you must go and what you must do. Fred, you will meet the three princesses at a place called AubreyVille."

"Ok."

"Frederick of Galvestein."

"Yes?"

"You will show them how to fight. They must practice here before going to the forest of jewels. If not, they will also be captured by the evil witch. The witch can deceive minds and is very clever."

"Elphias?"

"Yes, legendary hero?"

"I want you to tell them the prophecy."

"Ok, legendary hero."

The legendary hero stood up. "Let's take these princesses on an adventure they'll never forget."

"Oh" Before you go I have something to give you.

What is it? Said Frederick.

"Cell phones," said the Legendary Hero. These will help us contact each other in case of emergencies.

Wonderful!! Frederick and Elphias said in unison.

Off they went to their separate locations.

Meanwhile, back at the castle while the legendary hero was looking for his warriors…

# Chapter 14
# The Princesses of the Kingdom

Violet, Summer and Gloria were very sad that their oldest sister was captured.

They looked at each other. Why did that evil witch have to capture our sister? said Summer.

I wish there was a reason that she'd do this to us. Perhaps she was captured because she's more powerful than all of us, said Gloria.

Really? Said Summer.

I think it is true, said Violet. Something must be done about it.

How? Said summer.

For one thing we don't have powers, said Gloria.

That is true, said Summer. There's surely someone out there who could train us. But who?

We don't know.

Perhaps they'll find us before we can find them, said Gloria.

So what do you think we should do?

You bring a good point Gloria, said Violet. Perhaps we should put out papers around the kingdom so the heroes can find us.

That's a brilliant idea Violet, said Gloria. Let's do it.

They all went to work on their own projects. Gloria spoke with the guards, Violet created a banner and Summer thought of the words they should put on the banner. With each of their skills they were able to create what they wanted to share with the heroes.

Well Done sisters! Said Gloria. Now we wait for the heroes to show up.

# Chapter 15 The Warrior Arrives

The Legendary Hero was standing tall. "Thinking" when he saw something in the distance. I see something! He texted Frederick and Elphias.

Hmm... it seems I have a text from Elphias

"I just saw something out in the distance!"………

What do you see……

I see a banner!…….

Banner? What does it say?…..

## WE ARE THE PRINCESSES OF ISABEL WHO WAS CAPTURED!!! PLEASE FIND US IN THE CASTLE!! VISITORS WELCOME!! IF YOU'RE THE HEROES, COME QUICKLY!!!

I see it Legendary Hero!! I'm going to find them!!…..

Good luck Elphias…..

Thank you.

Elphias went straight to the castle. He saw two guards there.

Halt!! State your business!!

I'm Elphias. I'm a wizard.

A wizard you say?

Yes. Of course as Elphias bowed on his knee.

Welcome Elphias!!

Thank you sirs.

He opened the door and walked in.

# Chapter 16
# Elphias Meets the Princesses

The princesses were standing on the floor.

Hello Princesses!! I'm Elphias the wizard and I'm here to take you on a quest to find your sister who's been captured by the evil witch.

We all look forward to rescuing our sister. We are ready!!

Now wait a minute!!

What? sir Elphias, said summer.

You're not fit the way you are to stop her.

Just being yourselves isn't enough to stop the evil witch. That is why you need to be trained so you can stop her.

 I'm not the only one who can help you.

There is another warrior who will help you.

His name is Frederick of Galvestein who happens to be a swordsman.

Very intriguing, said Summer.

Indeed! said Elphias. Before we begin our quest is there a place I can stay? I think having something to eat is important.

Yes!! Of course, said Gloria. There is a place you can stay. Here inside the castle we have an extra room you can stay in.

Show me, said Elphias with confidence.

Of course, said Gloria with a smile.

As they continued up the stairs he saw many paintings of men who fought in a battle.

This is very interesting. Said Elphias

It is, said Violet. This will be your room.

Thank you princesses.

You're welcome Elphias.

I think before we retire for the night we should eat something.

Yes!! Of course Elphias!! I will speak to the guards and we'll think of something, said Gloria.

Gloria went to the guards at the front door.

Princess!! Said the guard. How can we help you?

Well. We need some food for our visitor.

Of course you do. Hmm… I believe we do have soldiers who get food from animals.

Interesting, said Gloria. I'll ask them.

She set out to find the general.  The general was standing by,  training his recruits.

GET DOWN AND GIVE ME TEN!!

Yes! Sire!!

Aah!! It's the princess!!Stand UP in Attention!! State your business princess.

Of course General, said Gloria with a smile. I hear you soldiers get food in the fields. Isn't that right?

Yes, princess, said a young man. We've killed deer, rabbits, and many other animals which we've cooked here in our camp.

Very fascinating, said Gloria. What do you have?

Well princess we do have meat. What do you have?

Hmm… I believe we carry corn, vegetables and fruit but not food.

Then it's settled!! You shall have our meat. I'm curious though. Why do you need food?

We have a visitor who's hungry.

Oh. That's very interesting. Is he the warrior that will train you on your quest?

Yes. How did you know?

We saw the banner in the sky and got to work to get your food.

Why thank you soldier!

Likewise, princess!!

Ok men!! You heard her!! Get the meat and let's go to the castle!!

Sir, yes Sir!

They returned to the castle and brought the meat!!

Dinner is Served Elphias!! Enjoy!!

Thank you Gloria!! This is wonderful. We get to meet here to enjoy this nice meal.

Indeed Elphias.

So ladies. Tell me about yourself.

The princesses blushed.

Oh Elphias. How does the meat taste?

It's amazing. Thank you.

Well since you've asked Elphias, we'd be happy to tell you about ourselves.

I'm Summer. I'm the youngest. What I love to do is read.

I'm Violet. I love the outdoors. I also love flowers.

I'm Gloria. I love to paint.

That's amazing ladies. I look forward to training you tomorrow.

Sleep well Elphias.

Thank you.

He's great isn't he, said Summer.

He is, said Gloria.

The girls went to sleep and had great dreams.

# Chapter 17
# The Prophecy

The next morning Elphias and the princesses woke up. Beautiful day isn't it ladies, said Elphias.

Indeed it is Elphias.

There's something I need to show you.

They followed Elphias to a meadow.

Elphias spoke.

To become like your sister, the most beautiful princess, who was captured by the wicked witch, you must journey to the land of Mystika. You will meet a swordsman and he will tell you where to find the shields, which you will defend yourself and fight in the light of Eric Thompson's domain. It is a beautiful and powerful place."

"It is sad that the evil witch has captured your sister. She is held in the witch's castle on the far side of the forest. But, don't worry, she won't be held forever. You will learn what you need to know while on this journey. The evil witch wants your mission to rescue your sister to fail. Once you have trained and practiced, you will enter the forest. It is filled with many dangers, but you will have a power that will light your way. As you come out of the forest, you will approach the evil witch's castle. As you enter the castle, a mysterious hero will join you. He is known as the legendary hero. It is through him that you will succeed in your quest. He will give you power unlike anything you have imagined. You must be bold and brave in order to free her."

Well said Elphias. Said Gloria.

You're welcome.

We have one thing to ask you before you go.

What is it Gloria?

We don't know where to go. Is there anything we can use to find our way? Like maybe a map?

Yes!! Of course!! A map you say. Give me one moment.

The Legendary Hero was waiting at the dark Forest when he saw a text from Elphias.

What's up?

I need your help......

What do you need?....

Remember what you told me about the journey for the princesses?.....

Yes. I remember. What about it?....

The princesses want a map to know where they're going. ......

You're right Elphias!! There is a map and I have it right here. I'll send you a picture. ......

Excellent.

The Legendary Hero sent the picture to Elphias.

Yes!! That's it.

I shall talk with the princesses so they don't get lost. Thanks again Legendary Hero. ......

My pleasure.

So.... What did you find out, Elphias? Said Violet.

I do have a map.

Let's see it.

Elphias showed the map on his phone. The princesses were perplexed after looking at it.

What is this Elphias?

It's an IPhone.

What's an IPhone?

I can see that this is confusing to you. The Legendary Hero has this device in a world where Eric Thompson lives.

Eric Thompson. Who's Eric Thompson?

Eric Thompson is a human being who lives on his own and has many friends. An iPhone is a special tool that shows technology and keeps track of many things. Kind of like this map. Since this is very confusing for you we'll do this a different way.

That would be wonderful.

# Chapter 18 The Map

The princesses were waiting in anticipation for what Elphias was about to show them. Elphias started to speak.

I'm sorry that you couldn't understand the map on my phone.

You said it, said Summer. So where do we go on our quest?

To say the least, said Elphias, you need to go to the keeper of the weapons. His name is Fred. He's not the swordsman but he is the man who takes care of the weapons. He lives in Aubreyville.

So this map can keep track of where we're going?

Yes. Do you see Aubreyville?

Yes. We do.

Great. Follow the map and you shouldn't get lost.

"Farewell, until I see you again."

"Farewell    Elphias.    Until    we    meet    again"

# Chapter 19
# The Keeper of the Weapons

Onward the three princesses traveled to find the swordsman in Mystika. He was easy to find since everyone knew him. As they approached the village, they came to the man as he was sharpening swords. Violet spoke up. "Excuse me Sir. We are trying to find the land of the evil witch. Do you know where it is?"

"Ah visitors. Welcome Violet, Summer, and Gloria. My name is Fred. To find the witch's castle you must have my swords and shields. The shields are found in the forest of jewels. I have a friend who can teach you everything you need to know how to use swords and shields. His name is Frederick of Galvestein. He is wise. He also knows the legendary hero who you will see later in your journey. The witch you will encounter can deceive minds. She is very powerful. But I am certain that you will triumph over her. Continue on to Eric's domain in the land of Mystika and you will find Frederick of Galvestein."

The three princesses continued on. Suddenly, Belinda appeared before them. "You who are coming to rescue Isabelle. I advise you to return back where you came from. There is no hope for you." Belinda laughed and then disappeared.

After the encounter, the three princesses continued on and easily found                          Eric's                          domain.

# Chapter 20
# Frederick of Galvestein

The three princesses approached a man in Eric's domain. Gloria asked, "Are you Frederick of Galvestein?"

"Indeed I am. Welcome. I can teach you everything you will need to know to rescue your sister. There is much you will need to learn. He asked the three of them to follow him to his shop. This is where you will practice with a sword. What you will learn first is to never be afraid, second to be brave and third to show light from your sword by saying the command "ignite". They practiced saying ignite and their sword glowed

"Step back and I will show you how to fight. You see that enemy with a smile on his face?

"We do."

"Hit him with your sword."

"Poof!"

"So, as you can see, you have an advantage over the enemy. But remember, you have to work together to defeat them. If you are surrounded, stand your ground and fight. To guard with your shield, keep it close to your body. You can block an attack. You won't be powerful yet, but you will have protection until you meet the legendary hero. Good          luck          on          your          quest."

# Chapter 21
# The Enemy

The three princesses continued on their journey. They came to the forest of jewels. It was dark and they couldn't see. They heard laughter from the enemy, one of whom said, "you can't cross this path."

Gloria answered, "Oh yeah? We can light up the forest." The princesses jointly said the command "IGNITE!" and the power was with them. With the way lit, they found the shields by the tree, right where they were supposed to be. They grabbed them and fought until there were no more enemies left. The path was now clear and there was still light within it.

The witch saw what happened and was furious. She yelled at the princesses. "You have killed my friends. Now you will face my wrath. I will see you in my castle."

Vanished!

There in front of them stood the legendary hero. "Well done princesses. You have fought valiantly. I am the legendary hero. Receive my powers to help defeat the evil witch. He touched the swords that they glowed so brightly. They were ready to fight Belinda.

# Chapter 22
# The Rescue of Isabelle

The three princesses entered the witch's castle. The evil witch attacked them but she couldn't match their amazing power.

Your swords are glowing! How?

Your reign is OVER Belinda! Their power was too much for Belinda to handle. Together they defeated Belinda.

The legendary hero came in and took Belinda to the dungeon, where they hoped she would never be heard from or seen again.

Well done sisters!!

I knew you would come and rescue me!

They happily untied the princess Isabelle.

The legendary hero stood with a pleasing look on his face. "Well-done ladies. You have completed your adventure. May you be happy forever. One last thing. You should consider looking for Eric Thompson.

# Epilogue

Everyone celebrated as they went their separate ways.

Well done Elphias and Frederick. You did very well training the princesses.

Thank you Demetrius. I thought we did very well. Training Eric is another matter.

Yes. It seems that he has no powers which makes him a vulnerable target to the villains.

That's true. What do you think about the princesses? Do you think we should marry them?

Marry them? I'm not so sure about that. What would they do? It's obvious they would live here in Eric's Domain along with everyone else.

Who would Eric marry?

I'm not sure. That's up to him. It seems that the princesses would love to do something like this. You Elphias me? I'm not sure. I think when they're ready they'll know. One thing is absolutely certain! Eric must be trained! By being trained he can defend himself.

What if he got captured?

If he got captured we would rescue him. After all, we have many heroes in our midst. I'll call Eric as I know his number.

Demetrius was on FaceTime.

I wonder who this is? Said Eric.

Hello?

Hello Eric.

You know my name?

Of course I do. And so does Braille, my master.

So why are you calling me?

I'm calling to tell you. You're becoming a superhero.

A superhero? I'm just a normal person. How can I become a superhero if I don't have weapons?

I will give them to you.

Ok.

I will talk to you very soon.

See you later.

................

*Meanwhile, back at the princesses castle……*

Mom! Dad! We're back!

The king and queen were very happy for their daughters' return.

How was the adventure girls? Said the queen.

We thought it went very well said Gloria. We received powers and met the famous Legendary Hero!

Did he help you?

Oh yes. He also told us about the famous Eric Thompson.

The queen looked in surprise.

Eric Thompson? Oh yes. Braille's wife told me about him.

How do you know about Eric? Said summer.

Because he is the chosen one. Do you think you'll marry the superheroes, including Eric?

The princesses looked at each other. Well we do know that we love the heroes who trained us.

Eric Thompson. Said Isabelle. He seems like the man I would marry. He's handsome, good looking and brave.

We all agree. We want to marry the superheroes. Until that time we will continue to keep the kingdom safe.

Well said my girls, said the king.

*Belinda   Back at the villains lair…..*

I was defeated but this is only the beginning. I will create my evil army and Eric's friends will be mine!! Ha ha ha.

## The End – Part 1

Characters

Legendary Hero:
the first superhero created by Spider-Man. The one who trained Elphias
and Frederick.

Spider-Man:
The Legendary Hero's Master and the one hero who created him.

Frederick: The man who was trained by the Legendary Hero. He also
became the warrior who could fight with a sword

Elphias: Trained by the Legendary Hero and became a wizard.

Violet: enjoys outdoors
Summer: loves reading books
Gloria: creative
Isabel: wisest of the sisters and most beautiful.
Spells:
Belashio
Strasinko
Dezmo
Shul: attack
Mela: shoot cords
Strasinko: attack
Dezmo: stun

# Part 2 - The Unfortunate Happenings of the Singles Ward

By Eric Thompson

## *Introduction*

Belinda was standing outside of the villain's lair thinking. She recalled her time that she captured the princesses oldest sister and held her captive. She was stopped from keeping Isabelle hostage. As she thought she realized something. She was missing something. Something she needed.

This is interesting! I was able to capture someone. It seems that I was captured. I shouldn't be captured again. I have many friends in the villain's lair. I think it's important that I find a partner who can join me on my quest of world domination. It's time for me to create my evil army.

Belinda walked into the villain's lair. The villains were enjoying themselves and then looked at Belinda.

Belinda. Welcome!!

Thank you ladies!!

What brings you here?

I'm here to tell you that I've decided to create an evil army to capture Eric Thompson and his friends.

That's a great idea. How will you do that?

Well I will first find a sorceress and then she and I will get Eric's friends on our side.

How do you know Eric so well?

Because the Legendary Hero talked about him. I will find Eric and his friends and make minions out of his friends. Ha ha ha.

The sky started to dim as their laughter reached the skies.

# Chapter 1
# Eric's Purpose

Eric was at home. He just woke up from his sleep. This is crazy. I just talked with the Legendary Hero for the first time and he wants me to be a superhero. I'm just a normal person. As a person I can be vulnerable to many villains. But as a superhero I can defend myself. I wonder why he's put me up to this quest. Perhaps I'm being trained for something more. Something important. Perhaps I do have a responsibility to lead my friends into a battle between good and evil. Perhaps the Legendary Hero has a purpose for me. For now I should live my life the way I am. I have many friends. Perhaps I should see them. They are my friends.
*And so Eric set out to find his friends.*

*Meanwhile in the Trista Dimension*
………………
Braille?
Yes honey?
What are you doing?
I'm preparing to send a capsule down to earth.
Why?
Come over here for a minute, Sheryl.
Sheryl walked over listening intently.
I'm sending Eric and his friends a message and only the legendary Hero can open it.
That makes sense. You want to prepare Eric for the big battle.

That's right. And he is going to become a superhero. I'm even going to go down to Eric's Domain soon.

Eric's Domain??? Remember what almost happened last time you were there trying to fix the computer? Yes. That's right. I was almost captured by Braze and his friends.

I can't bear to lose you again.

Relax honey. I'm not going anywhere.

Everything ready to go with the capsule?

Not quite. Just one call to make.

*Meanwhile in Eric's Domain*

………..

Ring…….

Hello? This is Demetrius

Hello Demetrius. This is your master Braille.

Braille! What's up?

I'm sending a capsule down to Eric Thompson.

Eric Thompson? The boy who will become a superhero?

That's correct. He's going to call you and he'll need your help.

Of course. I talked to him just recently.

Really?

Yes.

What did you say?

I told him he's going to become a superhero soon.

That's great to hear. I'm coming to Eric's Domain soon.

Sounds good. See ya. Bye.


Ok Braille! Your capsule is ready to be launched!

Excellent!! Eric!! Prepare yourself for a journey of power and wonder.

*The capsule soared through the sky.*

# Chapter 2
# The Capsule

Eric and his friends were hanging out when they saw something falling from the sky.

It's heading this way!! Said Eric.

Look out! They got out of the way just in time.

It was a big capsule. "What is this capsule? What is it doing here?" Eric said, "Maybe it has hidden powers."

"It might be a mystery."

"Let's open it."

"There might be a trap."

"Does it play music?"

"Where did it come from?"

"There is only one person who can open this capsule."

Everyone said at once, "Who?" and then replied, "We don't know."

"I might know," said Eric. "He is one of my best friends." Wait a minute!! There's a note on it!

What does it say Eric? Said one of the single adults.

It's a riddle. It says "I'm powerful but I'm not Eric. I spend time with his friends. Who am I?

Eric stroked his chin. "Of course. He is the only one I know who can open this capsule."

Who? The group asked, "Where can we find him?"

Eric responded, "He lives in my Domain." His name is "The Legendary Hero!"

How do we get to your domain?

Well. For one thing we can't get there because I don't have a lab like the Legendary Hero. I think it's possible for Spider-Man to take us there.

Spider-Man? He literally can't be reached because he doesn't exist.

"Excuse me!!" He does exist!!

He's just in another dimension.

A place that even I can't get to.

You mean to say you don't know how to get to your domain?

"There is a way!" Spider-Man can't get us to Eric's Domain. But the Legendary Hero can. In fact, he gave me his number!

Wow! That's awesome. For the record, sorry we got mad at you. We didn't need to do that.

It's ok guys. I forgive you. Let's talk with the Legendary Hero.

# Chapter 3
# The Legendary Hero and the Capsule

The Legendary Hero was in Eric's Domain when he heard his phone ring.

Let's see who it is. Oh. It's Eric. I should answer. Hello? This is the Legendary Hero.

Hi. It's Eric.

Hey Eric. What's up? You can call me Demetrius.

Sure. I need your help.

Anything for you Eric.

Can you come to my house?

Uh. Yeah. Sure. I'll come over.

Thanks, bye.

As he was coming over he thought, "I wonder what it is."

Who's that Eric? Said a single adult

There was someone in a black robe and black hood. Him? This is the Legendary Hero. His real name is Demetrius for short.

Well said Eric! I'm the Legendary Hero!

So… Eric. What do you need help with?

There's something we need to show you.

Show me the way!

Eric, the legendary hero and the group went back to where the capsule had settled on the ground.

The legendary hero said, "Well this is a big capsule indeed. Where did it come from?"

"It just dropped out of the sky."

Oh! I see a note. What does it say? It's a riddle. Yep. "I can open this."

The legendary hero gave a powerful blow to an exact spot on the capsule and it opened. The legendary hero reached in and pulled out a note and handed it to Eric. "What does it say?"

It says the following, "Welcome. You are all about to go on an adventure you will never forget. There will be mystery, danger, and bravery. Once you say "LET THE ADVENTURE BEGIN" you will be sent to an unknown land. As you set foot on the land you will be seeing things you have never seen before."

Oh. Before I go said Demetrius you all need wands if you want to transport to Eric's Domain.

# Chapter 4
# The Adventure Begins

"Wow." Said Eric. "This tells us what to expect—mystery, adventure, and bravery. All we need to say is "LET THE ADVENTURE BEGIN"."

With just a slight hesitation they all said it. Instantly they were transported to an unknown land.

"Whoa! Look at this." Eric said. "We are in a land full of dinosaurs and other animals."

"What are we doing here, Eric?"

"We are here to see the wildlife and their habitats—watch what they do."

"What will become of us?"

"Well, we need to be cautious and take plenty of pictures. Then we will meet someone."

"Who are we going to meet?"

"We will meet my friend and mentor of this land by the name of Scott."

"Scott? What does he do?"

"He's a scientist. He also knows how to survive in a place like this."

"Him? How can you be so sure?"

"I came here one time."

They went to see all the animals and especially the dinosaurs. When they finished taking pictures, they walked to the edge of the valley to speak to the scientist, Scott.

Scott shook hands with Eric. "Well, hello Eric. How are you?"

"I am doing well. These are my friends." Each in turn shook hands with Scott and said, "Nice to meet you Scott."

Eric looked at Scott. "So. What's new, Scott?"

"Well, I have discovered much about this land. It is dangerous, beautiful, and very adventurous."

"What will you do now Eric?"

"Head back home and spend time with my friends."

"Well     it's     nice     seeing     you     Eric."

# Chapter 5 Eric's Domain

We need to go home Eric! Said the single adults.

Before we get eaten!!

You got that right! Let's get out of here!!      Computer!!

Yes?

Take us home!!

Beginning transportation.

Whoosh!!


They made it safely back to Eric's Domain. .

Man Eric! Why does transportation have to seem so…. different??

Eric watched as they started to stagger and faint.

Why does this always seem to happen? Said Eric.

Eric spoke a command "Turn on Fans!!

The fans turned on. The single adults started to feel conscious and not as dizzy.

You guys all right?

We are now. Thanks Eric! Why does that transportation seem so dizzy?

I'm not sure. Perhaps I need to fix it. How do you want it to be?

Well we think it should be a beam. Who created this lab?

The famous Legendary Hero who we just met.

You really think he can fix this?

I think he can.

Where are we Eric? We are in my domain.

You have your own domain?

Yes. So tell me. What seems to be the problem with transportation?

Well for one thing when the computer speaks the floor rumbles. Second when we start transporting we see flashes of color and third when we land in the location we stagger and faint like you saw us do.

This makes a lot of sense. Perhaps we should talk with the Legendary Hero about it.

Where can we find him?

He's in my domain somewhere. I'll see if I can find him again.

Sounds great Eric. Thanks.

You're welcome!!

Eric went into the lab.

"Intruder Alert" "Intruder Alert"

Wait!! It's Me. Eric!!

Person approved, said computer.

"The Legendary Hero stormed in"

What is Going on? Oh. Eric. You're back!! I heard my threat detector go off. What's up?

Sorry to intrude. I need your help again.

Ok. How can I help?

Give me a second. Hey guys. It's safe! Come on in.

Eric!! Why are the single adults here again?

"He paused." They have some concerns.

Tell me.

Eric explained about the issues with transportation.

I see, said the legendary Hero with a concerned look on his face.

Why ask me? I didn't create this lab.

You didn't? Well then. Who did?

Spider-Man!

Spider-Man?

Yes.

Why?

He was my master.

Your master? Oh yeah! That's right. He created you and then he created this lab.

Well said Eric!

Then that means we need to talk to him.

You're right Eric.

How can we reach him?

It seems the only way to reach him is for the computer to track him down.

And how do I do that?

Eric! You have a lot to learn about this lab.

We all do? Said singles and Eric.

Yes.

They listened intently to what the legendary hero had to say.

# Chapter 6
# Eric and the singles
# Learn the Basics

Tell us what we need to know, Demetrius.

I will. When I started becoming the legendary

Hero I was alone and I didn't have any friends, so Spider-Man thought it would be best to get the superheroes together and see me. After they saw me Spider-Man gave me many powers, a lab, threat detector, computer that could locate anything, transportation device and powers that I could use. A lot of them include spells, powers and sword fighting.

That's very interesting, Demetrius. Said Eric. How can we use these powers?

Well that's simple Eric. Take a look at this.

He showed Eric a lightsaber, a wand and a sword.

This is really cool, said Eric.

It is Eric. Watch this. Computer!!

Yes?

Send some enemies.

He fought against them and when he touched them they poofed in smoke.

You have a chance to do it now Eric.

Sounds great. Computer!! Send enemies.

They came after him.

You Shall Not Prevail!!! They poofed in smoke.

Well done Eric! Now we will both fight an enemy with a saber.

Send an enemy with a saber! They fought.

Now Eric!!

Demetrius and Eric pushed the enemy with their hands, jumped over them and struck them with the saber.

Well done Eric!! I gotta say! You're really good with the saber and the sword.

Thank you.

There's two more powers for you to use.

What's that Demetrius?

Sorcerer and spells.

That's interesting. How does it work?

First you need to know how to be a sorcerer. Like me you will have a cape and just move your hands. It's kind of like telekinesis which gives you the ability to move objects. You can also create powerful spells that can disarm and attack powerful enemies.

That's cool.

Last but not least you will have a wand. There's many spells that are useful like belashio which can blast. Strasinko is the attacking spell. Dezmo is a stunning spell. Now you have a chance to fight me.

Strasinko!! I've attacked you. Dezmo!! You have been stunned. Now you try.

Dezmo!! Strasinko!!

Well done Eric!! You've officially learned how to fight with the sword and lightsaber as well as learning to be a sorcerer and using a wand. Well done.

I think it's time to find Spider-Man.

That's a good idea Eric.

Computer!!

Yes?

Find Spider-Man!!

Locating Spider-Man….. He's in New York!! Shall I call him for you?

No. But please send me his number.

Searching……

The phone number showed up.

Thank you computer.

You're welcome.

Thanks for everything Demetrius.

It was my pleasure. Until we meet again Eric Thompson.

………………………

Wow Eric!! We learned a lot from the Legendary Hero.

Everyone was standing outside of Eric's Domain.

Yes. We did. It's not the end though. It's only the beginning. Before we go to the stake center we should find Spider-Man to help you fix the problem with your transportation issue.

That's a great idea!!

I'll find him. I have his number.

The computer gave you his number?

Yep.

I'm going to call him now.

Ring…….

# Chapter 7
# Eric calls Spider-Man

Hello? This is your friendly neighborhood Spider-Man.

Hey Spidey.

Who's this?

The famous Eric Thompson.

Eric Thompson? I know all about you!

You do?

I knew you since the time that I met the Legendary Hero.

You did?

Yes.

But how did you know me?

I've been watching you Eric.

You've been watching me?

As a matter of fact, I have. You love superheroes!!

I do!!

It seems you've called me about something. What is it?

Well Spider-Man, it seems that my single adult friends have had problems with the transportation device.

Transportation device?

Yes. They say it rumbles, makes them dizzy and then they faint.

Oh really?

Yes. What can be done about it so it doesn't make them dizzy?

I don't know Eric. I didn't create the lab.

You don't know? But. Demetrius said you did create Eric's Domain and the lab.

There's a lot you don't know about. Something that happened from the beginning when I met my master.

Ok. Can you come down to my domain and tell me more about this story?

Of course. I'll be right there. See you, bye.

Eric and his friends stood in awe.

We didn't know Spider-Man had a master.

Neither did I, said Eric.

# Chapter 8
## Spider-Man Speaks with Braille

Spider-Man was sitting on top of a building in New York.

This is very interesting. So Eric wants to know more about my master? He also wants to know how to fix the transportation problem. I can't fix it but I know that Braille can. After all, he's the one who created it long ago. What would Braille do if I called right now? What would he say? Would he be disappointed? Why do I even need him?

As Spider-Man thought about his master Braille he remembered what Eric said. "We need help with the transportation device".

Yes. That's right! I should call Braille.

And so he did.

Ring…..

*In another dimension called Trista…..*

Braille was on his computer when he got a call. He saw Spider-Man's caller ID show up.

"Why is Spider-Man calling me?"

Does he know that I have to figure out my father's legacy since he died long ago?

*New York………*

It seems he's not answering. I'll have to leave a voicemail. Hi Braille, this is Spider-Man. I need your help!! I recall you created Eric's Domain but it seems that Eric Thompson and his friends are having problems with the transportation device you created. Is it possible that you can come there and help with it? Talk to you soon, bye.

*Trista……*

It seems that Spider-Man has left me a voicemail.

He listened to it.

Oh!! This is very interesting indeed. I had a feeling that name would come up one day. Eric Thompson. Eric Thompson! Spider-Man told me that name a long time ago. He said that one day a man named Eric Thompson would show up and that he would need my help. I think that it's time now to meet him for the first time. He deserves to know what happened in the beginning with my father and how I turned into a sorcerer. I will do this. I'm going to tell my wife about this. She deserves to know this. I'll spend one week with Eric and his friends so he knows the whole story about me. That transportation device needs to be fixed anyway.

Braille went into the house and talked with his wife.

Honey!!

Yes Braille?

I have some news!!

What kind of news?

You remember that man Spider-Man was talking about?

Oh yes!! I remember!! Eric Thompson. Isn't that right?

Yes.

What about Eric Thompson?

He needs my help.

Your help? Does he even know you?

No. He doesn't.

Then why go to him?

Because he needs help with a transportation device. I'll only be gone for a week.

Haven't you forgotten I'm pregnant with two children?

Yes. I'm aware. I'll be back before the babies are born. It's not like I'm going to be gone forever.

Promise me you won't tell Eric anything about us.

I promise. Ok. I'm gonna get going.

Good luck!

Thanks honey.

Braille called Spider-Man back.

*New York……..*

Ring….. Hello this is your friendly neighborhood Spider-Man.

Spider-Man!!

Braille!! It's nice to hear your voice. I thought I wasn't going to hear from you.

Yes. I did get your message. Thanks again. I'm coming!!

You're coming to Eric's Domain? Isn't that dangerous since all the villains are trying to capture you after you had your revenge on the villain who killed your father?

I know the risks. I'm only staying for one week to tell Eric and his friends my story as well as fix the transportation device.

Does your wife know?

Yes. She's ok with it.

Ok then. I'll let Eric know you're coming.

No!! You don't need to do that. I'll tell him myself in person.

Ok. Be careful, Master!

I will! I give you my word.


*Meanwhile, Back in Eric's Domain……*


Spider-Man hasn't gotten back to me in such a long time that I wonder if he forgot about me.

Suddenly the phone rang. It was Spider-Man.

It's about time!! Hey Spidey! Any luck?

As a matter of fact. Yes. Someone is coming to you.

Who?

I can't say.

Why not?

I just can't but you'll know very soon. They're on their way.

Great. Thanks again Spidey.

It was my pleasure Eric.

................

Eric was deep in thought. The singles were looking at him confused.

What are you thinking about Eric?

I'm thinking about Braille. I've never heard of him. I also realize that there's something else I'm missing.

Like what?

Well I know that I've learned everything from Demetrius and that I've met him. Demetrius was looking at Eric from a distance.

You're right Eric. There is something missing.

And what would that be Demetrius?

My warriors.

Your warriors? You mean to say you trained two of them?

Yes. I did.

That's really interesting, Demetrius. So are you saying that they actually live here? With you?

You got that on very well Eric. Would you all like to meet them?

We absolutely would.

That would be nice but we first should go to the stake center. You wanted a play right?

Yes. We did. Promise us after we go to the stake center and back NO more transportation!! Please!!

I promise!!

# Chapter 9
# The Rise of Daisy

Belinda was flying.

I must find an evil sorceress for my quest of world domination. Ah. There's someone. She spoke in a loud voice:

You have been chosen. I will give you the power, like me, to take over the world, but there is a price that you will pay if you let someone defeat you. Be wary of Eric. He is so powerful that no one can defeat him. It is your destiny to bring Eric to me and together we can use our power to be rid of his greatness. The world will be dark as I trap Eric in my dungeon. So, you shall find him and carry out my wishes.

The woman said, "No, I will not fight Eric."

Belinda landed in the grove of trees where she was.

She ran.

You have No choice, my dear. Shay!

She fell on the ground. Nooo!!

Zaluma!

The woman smiled at Belinda. I'm Daisy!

And I'm Belinda!

So. What brings you here Belinda?

Well. I'm here to build my army and take over the world. I also have two evil brothers. Malcolm and Braze.

So you need a sorcerer?

Yes. I do.

Where can you find one?

That's pretty easy since I have a place just like Eric's Domain.

Eric's Domain? What's Eric's Domain?

That is where they have a lab that has everything including a computer that can take anyone anywhere. I live at the villain's lair. The villain's lair has all the traps for the heroes as well as many villains. They also have a locator for villains of every kind.

So where have you found a villain?

In Ashello. It's a different place but I know I'll find who I'm looking for. What's the sorcerer's name?

Krell.                    He's                    a                    sorcerer.

# Chapter 10
# The Stake Center

They transported again and after they got dizzy Eric cast a new spell of his own to catch the single adults before they fainted.

Meesto!! They slowly fell down. After a moment they got up again.

How did you do that Eric? That was amazing!

I created a new spell that slowed you down. I don't know if there's any sign of danger but I'll let you know. Wait here!

Sounds great.

He looked around and to his amazement found the place deserted. He immediately thought. *Whoa. Where is everyone? I need to find out what is going on.*

Eric calls out, "Is anyone here?

Suddenly he saw an evil sorceress standing nearby.

Eric looked at her in surprise. Who are you? What are you doing here?

The evil sorceress said, I'm Daisy. I have come here to take over the world. Ha, Ha, Ha. My plan is simple. I will turn your friends into my minions."

Eric ran back outside. "Guys. I have some bad news."

Josh has a concerned look on his face. "What is it?"

"There's an evil sorceress in the building!"

"Oh no! How is that possible?"

"I don't know. You can't face her alone." "Ok. Follow me."

"Are you serious, Eric?"

"I am serious. Ok, here's the plan. Just watch what I do. No one can defeat me."

They went inside the building and faced the evil sorceress Daisy.

"Ah, Eric, you brought the single adults with you. Now I will make you all my minions. Ha, Ha, Ha."

Eric cast a spell by saying, "STRASINKO!" Daisy was pushed back. "Eric, you are very powerful. I thought the legendary hero was powerful."

"He is. He can be anyone"

"Oh, you can't be serious."

"I am. You will never succeed Daisy. You can't possibly overcome me. I want you to be good."

"I can't."

"Why?"

"An evil witch named Belinda gave me these powers."

"You can't be serious, Daisy."

"I am serious, Eric."

"So, you are on my side now, right Daisy?"

"Yes, I am."

"Why the sudden change?"

"Because I like to be good."

"You tried to make minions out of the single adults. Why?"

"So, I could have extra protection from other forces."

"Ok, Daisy. You've convinced me. Tell me what happened."

"Ok, Eric."

Well Eric, there was an evil witch named Belinda. She was following me in a grove of trees. I tried to run but she was too quick. She said she had an evil plan and that I would help her. I said no, she didn't give me a choice and I became her sorceress. The spell she cast was Zaluma which made me do her bidding.

That's very interesting. When the spell was cast what was the transition like?

Well it felt bad at first and then I started to have an evil smile. Then I did whatever she wanted and I loved it.

Eric looked concerned. Did she say where she was going?

"Recalling her memory she said", Ashello!

Ashello? Did she mention who she was seeing?

Krell!

Who's Krell?

I don't know.

What should we do Eric? Said the singles.

"We must go back to my domain."

"Why?"

"You, my friends, have much to learn before facing the sorcerers.

"Are you sure?"

"Yes. We must leave now."

Eric, Daisy and the singles ward left to go back to Eric's domain.

# Chapter 11
# The Power of Heroes

Everyone got back to Eric's domain and Eric cast his spell to slow down the dizzying.

I don't know how you do that Eric, said Daisy. It's amazing.

Thank you Daisy. I think there's a couple people we need to meet.

Frederick was standing by.

Eric? Is that you?

Frederick of Galvestein walks over. "

It is. How do you know my name?" Demetrius told me all about you.

I'm flattered. Thanks.

Ah! This must be the single adults. Welcome! This is the place where you will learn everything that's required to defeat evil. I have swords, wands, light sabers, and many other things that you will need."

"Thank you, Frederick."

The singles looks at Eric "So, how will we train?"

"There are many things you need to know before training."

"Like what?"

"There is much that can be learned from the book, *Survival and what it means to be a fighter.*

"What is survival?"

"Survival is the instinct of staying alive. Survival is the way to be victorious."

"What does it mean to be a fighter?"

"Fighting can keep enemies from succeeding."

"How?"

"Having courage and bravery."

"What is courage?"

"Courage is standing strong and proving justice to anyone that stands in the way."

Elphias showed up. Hi everyone. I'm Elphias the wizard. I too was trained by Demetrius.

It's nice to meet you Elphias.

# Chapter 12
## Eric meets Braille for the first time

All the singles and Eric were talking with Elphias Frederick and Demetrius when they saw a sorcerer transport on the patio. He wore a yellow cape with a blue mask.

Look!! Said Demetrius. It's our Master! Braille!

They kneeled as a token of respect.

It's been too long, said Braille. Too long.

For many years we've had these heroes here. Spider-Man, Elphias, Frederick of Galvestein Demetrius and of course the Chosen one, the famous Eric Thompson!!

Me? Said Eric in surprise?

Yes! You Eric!! The man who will defeat villains as well as train a boy named Sam!

You ask much of me sir! Said Eric.

And it's only the beginning!

It is?

It is.

I've known you for so long. Even before you met Daisy and Demetrius.

You did?

Yes. You Eric have a responsibility. I trust Demetrius trained you well?

He did. Now I'm training these single adults to prepare for a big battle that Daisy told me about.

Daisy!! Said Braille with a scowl! What are you doing here? I could banish you from this realm.

Cut her some slack Braille! She's on my side now.

Oh really?

Really.

Are you sure Daisy?

Yes sir. I am.

Good.

I hate to intrude master said Demetrius, but have any villains seen you since your revenge on your father's death?

There was only one villain who saw me.

Who was it?

Braze!

Belinda's oldest brother?

That's right.

It was his father who killed my father and he wants to have revenge on me.

You know he'll look for you right?

I'm well aware.

And the fact that you have a family is so much worse!

Why did you say that Demetrius? Now Eric knows. And I promised my wife I wouldn't mention anything about it.

I'm sorry Master.

Do you have a family Braille? Said Eric

A boy and a girl.

It's my promise to you. I won't tell anyone. Not even Belinda.

You won't tell her, will you Daisy?

I promise.

Good. Braille?

Yes Eric?

We need your help!

Oh yeah. Something to do with transportation?

Yes. Can you fix it?

Sure.

They all walked into the lab.

…………

So what seems to be the problem? Said Braille

Well for one thing when the computer speaks the floor rumbles. Second when we start transporting we see flashes of color and third when we land in the location we stagger and faint like Eric saw us do.

Oh really?

He slowed us down when we started to fall.

Whoa!! We didn't know that, said Elphias and Demetrius. What was the spell?

Meesto.

Meesto? That's interesting you created it. What happened? It slowed them down.

Very impressive Eric said Braille. So you just cast the spell by yourself? With no one around?

Yep.

That's awesome. Okay. So the problem is the floor rumbles, there's flashes of color and third they stagger and faint.

Correct.

Hmm…

Let me try something. Computer!

Yes?

Transportate.

It started to transport. He looked at it.

It seems you're right Eric. How to fix it?

They tell me that they just want to get beamed to the location.

I think it's possible. The only way to fix the problem is to see how it's modified. Let's see the settings. Oh My!! No wonder it isn't right.

What do you see?

The controls aren't in the correct sequence. Someone must've been tampering with it.

In another dimension far away………

Oh my Gosh!! Said Braze!

What? What is it? Said an evil woman named Lucy.

I just saw Braille!!

Really? Where?

Eric's Domain!! I got you now Braille!! After so many years!! Lucy! Get the villains!!

With pleasure!!

………………..

Oh No!!

What is it Braille? Said Eric.

I've got to get out of here!

Now?? But you just got here!

I know Eric! Villains have been trying to track me all these years.

Demetrius!! Keep watch of the computer!!

I will master!

…………..

Noooooooo!!!!!

I almost had him!!

There will come a day I will find you and you will be mine!

Gone Braze?

Gone Lucy!

Where did he go?

I don't know but I will have my revenge one day.

………………

Eric, the heroes Demetrius and Braille made it safely out of the shed.

Oh my goodness! I never imagined that Braze would find me that easily. He's never found me in my dimension. And he can't because it's heavily protected.

Who is Braze? Said Eric

Braze is the son of the man I killed.

You killed his father?

I had to! He killed my father!

But why kill?

I didn't stab him. He was an evil sorcerer. I struck him with a lightsaber.

That makes sense. Like a protector of peace.

Well said Eric. I can't stay.

I want you to stay!

I want to know more about you.

Someday I will return. Until that day Demetrius and Spider-Man will always be with you.

Spider-Man?

Yes.

He is my master Eric.

Really Demetrius?

Yes. And Braille is Spider-Man's master.

I'm really astounded Braille. So what about the computer?

The computer? It's too dangerous. Braze will find you and when he does you will be his captive. He's more powerful than Malcolm. Malcolm is someone I'm sure you'll defeat.

Thanks for the confidence Braille. Will I ever see you again?

I think you will.

How can you be so sure?

Because I live in a dimension called Trista. The computer can also call me. It won't be dangerous to ask requests but it will if you try to change the settings. The last time I tried to change the settings I saw a portal and villains came rushing through it. I narrowly escaped.

Eric had determination on his face. So where did that portal come from?

Christanova!

I will go there and face him one day. I give you my word!

He's too powerful Eric!

I'll be powerful enough!

If I recruited Belinda and her other sorcerer friends including a family with powers we'd be unstoppable.

I also would be ready to train Sam as you mentioned. He would be the one to defeat Braze!

You've got this figured out way out in advance Eric.

I have. I just know because I can see the future. Farewell Braille! I hope that your children are as powerful as you.

Thanks for the confidence. Farewell everyone. Porifay to Trista!

He instantly vanished.

# Chapter 13
## Krell and Belinda

Krell looked upwards. *I wonder why this witch is flying in the sky. Things aren't going so well. Rone and Crystal always seem to overcome me every time. Not even my friends can stop Rone. He is too powerful.*

Belinda landed on the ground.

Krell asked, "Who are you?"

"I am Belinda the evil witch."

"What brings you here to the land of Ashello?"

"Revenge!"

"Ah! You want to take over the world."

"Yes, I do!"

"Well I am happy you are here. There are two heroes I have tried to defeat."

"Who are they?"

"Their names are Rone and Crystal. I am Krell, the most powerful person in this land. I have lots of powers."

"Well, Krell, it's nice to meet you."

"I have a plan."

"What is your plan Belinda?"

"Well, I need minions. Lots of minions. In order to take over the world I need to have an army that can help us succeed in our quest of world domination."

"And who will you be fighting Belinda?"

"Eric Thompson."

"Are you serious? He's very powerful."

"Well, so am I. "

"So, what do you propose we do, Belinda?"

"I want you to bring Rone and Crystal out of their hiding place and bring them to me."

"I shall do as you ask." Krell rode away on his horse to get Rone and Crystal.

Crystal, as she approached Rone, said, "Oh Rone."

Rone looked at Crystal. "I am so happy you have stopped Krell."

"Well, what can I say? I'm a hero. How often do you practice with your sword Rone?"

"I practice a lot."

"Well, I am happy to be with you."

"Ah, what a lovely surprise." Krell said.

Rone asked, "What are you doing here?"

Krell responded. "Come and get me if you can. Ha, Ha, Ha."

Rone faced Crystal and said, "Get after him Crystal." Rone and Crystal rode swiftly after Krell but stopped abruptly when they saw Belinda.

"Well done Krell. You have brought them here to me."

"Who are you?" Rone asked.

"Oh, little hero, I am Belinda, the evil witch."

Rone looks at Crystal and shouts, "Take her on Crystal." She began casting her magic at Belinda but the witch blocked her every move. Rone raised his sword to strike Belinda but her countering blow blasted Crystal who was grabbed by Krell. Belinda then used her powers to remove Rone's sword and shield. Krell grabbed Rone.

"Throw them in the dungeon," commanded Belinda as she laughed and laughed. "Now that they are out of the way I can summon our army."

"Villains of the house of villains come forth." They all appeared.

Krell with a grin on his face said, "This is our time to reclaim what's ours. We will start the battle to take over the world, and then when they feel all hope is lost, victory will be ours." Belinda, Krell and the villains were all very happy and excited.

Belinda, standing at the front, said, "Let us begin."

Krell, watching Belinda, said, "What do we do?"

"We wait. Eric and his friends will come, and when they do, they will be at the mercy of our army. Eric will be mine! Ha, Ha, Ha."

The clouds closed in and everything went dark. Their scheme had just begun to evolve, but little did they know how powerful the friends of Eric                          would                          be.

# Chapter 14
# The Training Begins

"Wow, Eric! That was amazing to know about Braille wasn't it?" Said the singles.

Yes. It was.

We should use that Porifay spell next time.

Yes. We should.

"Now what about me?" asked Daisy.

"Well, what you have to do is practice your magic as much as you can. You leave the battling of Belinda to me."

"To you? She is so powerful."

"So, am I. Singles Ward?"

"Yes Eric?"

"Do you remember everything I mentioned to Elphias and Frederick?"

"Yes, we do," said Josh.

"Ok, then. Watch and learn. Elphias?"

"Yes Eric?"

"Attack me."

"Ok, STRASINKO! DEZMO!

"Did you see that my friends? I stunned him. Strike me again."

"Ok. STRASINKO!

"Nice shot, Elphias. You got me. Now point your wand at me." Elphias shot the spell and Eric blocked it. "Did you see how I blocked that my friends?"

"Yes, we did."

"Ok, now it's your turn. Say, Strasinko.

"STRASINKO!"

"Well done. You have officially used an attacking spell. Now you are ready to take on an enemy. Computer?"

"Yes Eric?"

"Send Belinda."

"Belinda?"

"Yes." As soon as the computer said those words, she appeared.

"Eric., watch out! Said Daisy.

This is not the real Belinda. The real one will be much worse."

"Ok. Belinda attack me!

Belinda pointed her wand and commanded, **SHAY**!

Eric countered with, STRASINKO! Their spells collided. "You will not succeed, Belinda. Watch this my friends." Eric powered his hands to the extent of the force and blasted Belinda.

"COMPUTER. STOP!" Belinda disappeared.

"Holy cow, Eric! That was amazing! How did you do that?"

"Do you remember that I am the chosen one?"

"Yes, we do."

"Great. Now it's your turn.

"What do you prefer to use, a wand, a sword, or a lightsaber.?"

"I would like a lightsaber."

"Ok, then. Hey Frederick ?"

"Yes, Eric?"

"I want you to find a lightsaber." Frederick went into the shop, found one and handed it. "Ok. Let me have the lightsaber. I have something to show you before you use it."

"Ok Eric. Just tell me what to do."

Eric said, "COMPUTER."

"Yes Eric?"

"SEND OVER A DARK LORD. ."

"Ok." There in front of Eric stood a dark lord. Lightsabers were ignited and the battle was on. The dark lord tried to slice Eric in ribbons, but Eric was too fast for him. Sparks flew as they fought until Eric back flipped over him and struck him down.

"Eric, that was amazing."

"Thank you. Here is the lightsaber." Eric hands the lightsaber to the single adult "You are ready to be trained. Turn it on."

"Do you feel it? Do you feel the power?"

"I do. It feels great."

"Now you have a chance to fight me. I'll take it easy on you. They fought. Their lightsabers clashed against each other.

"You are doing well. Now, try to focus your energy on blasting me away. I won't do anything to resist. They used both of their hands and blasted at Eric. But, due to the force Eric had, he fell back and landed strongly on his feet. "Good job, Well done. Now, Frederick

"Yes, Eric?"

"I want you to fight me."

"Ok." Frederick had brought his sword with him and Eric picked up his own. As they came together, the blades crashed against each other and then when the battle was almost over Eric tripped Frederick and he fell down.

"That my friends is how to defeat an enemy. Well done everyone."

Everyone was pleased with what they had learned. "Now, what do we do Eric?"

"We are going to practice. We will use magic and everything else that I showed you." The practice continued for many hours.

"You are ready to defeat Belinda, Krell, and their army."

Singles asked, "They have an army, Eric?"

"Yes, they do."

"So, what do we do?"

"We need to go to the land of Ashello and face Belinda and Krell. Can you take us there?"

"Yes, just say the word."

"My friends. We are going to Ashello to rescue Rone and Crystal. Are you ready?"

"We are."

"Great.

"Are you comfortable with the lightsaber?"

"Yes, we are."

'Single Adults, are you all ready to come with me?"

"Yes, we are."

"Do you have swords, shields, and wands and do you feel the power?"

"Yep."

Eric then had everyone gather in a tight group. They had everything in their bags. Now say Porifay to the land Ashello. Wands at the ready. *Porifay To The* LAND OF ASHELLO." They were transported to Ashello.

# Chapter 15
## The Fear of Rone and Crystal

"Rone?"

"Yes Crystal?"

"I am trapped in this dungeon."

"So am I."

"How will we get out?

Crystal shakes the bars. "I can't open them. They are magic protected. What will we do Rone?"

"I don't know. What can we do?"

"I have a feeling that Eric and his friends are coming here to rescue us."

"Are you sure?"

"I am absolutely sure."

"Yes, I knew there was hope."

"What do we do now?"

"We wait. Eric will come, and when he does, he will free us."

"What should we do about Belinda?"

"Avoid her. We must do our best to defeat Krell. We are not alone. I know that we will be free. Belinda and Krell have had their fun but I have courage. Let us wait until Eric arrives. When he gets here we will be ready. My sword and shield will come back to me." They waited and waited and waited...

Belinda looked at Krell. "Oh, it is so nice to have you with me. We will take over this war and we will be victorious."

"Yes, I believe you. Let's go see Rone and Crystal."

Belinda, with a wicked smile on her face, said, "Well, Well, Well. Rone and Crystal trapped. Ha, Ha, Ha."

Crystal screams. "Let us out!"

Belinda replied, "We will never let you out. Even you, Rone, can't overcome my power."

Rone said, "I'll make you a deal, Belinda."

"And what will that be?"

"If you let me go, I will fight Krell."

"Are you serious? You can't take him on without using Crystal's magical powers."

"Well. You are right. I can't wait to see Eric get here and kick your butt."

"Oh, Rone. Such courage you have. It seems that Eric and I have had countless battles. He may have defeated me before, but I have become more powerful than ever. Even if he tried he wouldn't be able to defeat me."

"You're bluffing Belinda. You can't possibly match his amazing power. I have heard he is the chosen one and the most powerful person ever."

"Ok, Rone and Crystal, I shall wait until they arrive and then they will be at my mercy."

"You just wait, Belinda. When we get out of here you will face justice."

Belinda looked at Krell. "I can't stand anymore of this. Let's get out of here."

"With pleasure."

Belinda looked startled. "Krell, did you hear that?"

# Chapter 16
## The Rescue of Rone and Crystal

The group arrived in the same position that they were in when the computer transported them to the land of Ashello. Josh let out a sigh of relief. "We made it." That was so much easier than transporting!!

The group looked around in horror. "Oh, no. There are so many of them. What do we do now Eric?"

"Stand your ground. Remember everything that I taught you. You are stronger and more powerful than you realize."

"Ah, there they are," said Belinda. Such a pleasure to meet the famous Eric Thompson. Nice of you to stop by." Belinda did not hesitate. She yelled. "Army, attack." The war started.

In the midst of the fighting Belinda noticed Daisy and called out. "Daisy, I thought you were going to take care of Eric?"

Daisy shouted back. "I failed."

"Enough of your excuses. I will punish you."

Eric shouted above the clamber. "Daisy, free Rone and Crystal. I will handle Belinda."

"No, you can't betray me Daisy."

"That is where you are wrong, Belinda."

"How did you turn her to the good side?"

Eric appreciated Belinda's frustration. "I persuaded her because the blow knocked her out and then she told me how you overcame her with such a little spell that she was under your control and she joined me."

"You will not prevail Eric." The fighting continued... "**SHAY!**" ... "**STRASINKO!**"

While Eric and the group were fighting Belinda, Daisy ran to the dungeons where Rone and Crystal were imprisoned. As she entered the tunnel leading to the dungeon entrance she heard a loud command. "You will go no farther."

"Oh, and what makes you think you can stop me?"

"I am Krell, Lord of Ashello. I have much evil that you can't overcome."

"My name is Daisy the sorceress."

"You? A sorceress? You seem to be a normal human being."

Daisy waved her wand at Krell and said, "ZARMEL". The spell caused Krell to fall over backwards. Daisy looked at Rone and Crystal. "I have come to free you."

Rone said, "Thank you, whatever your name is."

"I am Daisy, the most powerful sorceress." Daisy removed the magic on the bars when she said, "DISPERSE". Crystal and Rone were now free and got their powers back.

Rone found his sword and shield. "Let's go back to the battle." Rone went to the stables to get his horse he rode off to face the enemies.

# Chapter 17
# Eric and Belinda

Belinda was fighting mad. "I can't stand you Eric. You overcame my plan. My army is falling because you trained the single adults so well. I could not have done anything more to be even with all that you have."

"Belinda, you can't win. Even with all your power you can't possibly overcome me. I may be Eric, but the legendary hero is with me."

"Him? He's just a ghost."

"No. He stays in my home for protection."

Belinda said, "I'll give you one chance to surrender and then we won't bother you anymore. We will play video games and see all the friends that you know from Facebook and the people you associate with. We could rule the world together and nothing would stand in our way. There would be no rules. Just fun."

"Belinda, you have a lot to learn about life. It isn't based on video games and friends. It's about enjoying experiences and being independent. Eventually, if you have the courage, you can live on your own.

"Enough, Eric. I am tired of your lectures. Now, you will be my captive." Belinda pointed her wand and yelled, "**INCARCERATO!**"

**BELASHIO!!**

They cast their spells at the same time. They both got blasted away. Eric recovered quickly and said **DEZMO!!**

It stunned her.

Get ready Crystal. **STRASINKO!!**

The wand fell out of Belinda's hand.

Crystal bound her up. The war was won.

# Chapter 18
# The Victory

"You did it, Eric. You defeated Belinda."

"No Rone, you and Crystal did. I couldn't believe that she was so powerful. Her blasting spell pushed me a bit. It took a lot to convince her the truth of living a good life. She would never admit it. For that, she would always be evil forever. She even offered to accept my surrender so she could live a good life with my friends and I. But why would I trust her? She had a plan. And, if she succeeded, the world would be dark forever."

"Now, what do we do with Krell?

"That's a good question, Rone. Crystal?"

"Yes, Eric?"

"I want you to put Krell in prison. Can you do that?"

"I shall do as you ask, Eric."

"I am very proud of you my friends. You fought bravely. I couldn't believe the army that was there to fight us. If it wasn't for your courage and bravery we wouldn't have succeeded against them. A long time ago I had a dream that I possessed incredible powers from a master of mine—he gave me everything. These villains we fought against have grown stronger and stronger and in so doing have been able to capture me. They had a plan to capture me first so they could take over the world. They did capture me many times, but I had something with me that helped me escape:

"What was it?"

"It was the same device that enabled me to transport from one place to the other."

Josh said, "You did well Eric. Thank you."

Eric looked at all the faces of those who had fought so bravely. "Thank you all for believing in me."

"So, what do we do now Eric?"

"We go home. Goodbye, Rone and Crystal. I hope to see you again someday. And Rone?"

"Yes, Eric?"

"Let no evil stop you. Remember, you have the sword and I believe in you."

"Thank you, Eric."

"You're welcome. Remember, feel the power you have. Use it. Guard and remember to give justice. Ok, my friends. Let's go home."

Wands    at    the    ready!    *"PORIFAY    TO    ERIC'S    HOUSE"*

# Chapter 19
## The Adventure Ends

Eric and the group were happy to be home. "Thank you, single adults. You were so brave."

"Thank you, Eric.

"You're welcome. I want you to know that I will always be around. Whenever you need me, just call me. I will always be here.

Daisy asked, "What will become of Rone and Crystal?"

"Don't worry. They are powerful together. They will always be ready for anything. The sword that Rone has will vanquish any enemy.

Josh asked for the whole group. "So, what do we do now?"

"Nothing. You can go back to your old lives. This adventure has ended. But don't worry we will see each other again soon. I'll see you at the singles activities."

"Eric?"

"Yes?"

"Thank you for training us."

"We couldn't have done this without you. I enjoy your friendship. All of you. Well, I guess this is goodbye."

So, the single adults left Eric's house and there was peace in the world once again.

# Epilogue

*Meanwhile, Back in Trista…….*

It's so good to be back!! That was too close!!

It was Braille!! How did it go?

Well. To say the least I did meet Eric but I didn't have a chance to get to know him that much. I did talk about myself. I tried to fix the computer again when I saw an error message. Braze was ready to capture me at that moment. I did get out of the lab though. I will return to Eric's Domain!

When do you think you will go back? I will be there again when Eric has defeated Malcolm.

That's a great time honey. The twins will arrive in a week.They will be of age when Eric starts training Sam.

That's perfect honey. I'll wait until the time is right and then I'll tell him what happened with my father.

Sounds great.

I have a feeling when the time is right we'll be able to destroy Braze's computer and he'll never be able to track us again.

Feeling confident aren't you?

For the first time in my life I feel things are going in the right direction.

Couldn't have said it better Braille.

## The End of Part 2

# Part 3 - Belinda's Revenge

By Eric Thompson

## *Introduction*

Previously there was peace in the world when Eric returned home. But then something happened. Something Eric never expected to happen. This is also the time that Eric became evil. Can good conquer evil?

# Chapter 1
# Belinda Escapes

As the wicked witch Belinda sits in prison, she wonders. *I can't believe I'm stuck here. I wish I were out.* And, she begins to hatch a plan. *If only Eric was like me. We would be unstoppable. Now how do I get out of these bars? I remember a spell that I used which made everyone do my bidding. It is powerful.*

Belinda calls out from her cell. "Oh Guard!"

The guard responds. "Quiet."

"Come closer, Guard."

"I said be quiet."

Belinda thought, *if I can't get that guard to come to me voluntarily, I'll use a spell to make him come to me.* She pointed her wand at him and whispered "**ZALUMA**". The guard was now under her control and her plan was perfected.

She said to the guard, "Free me."

"Yes ma'am."

"My name isn't ma'am; it's Belinda."

"Of course, Belinda."

As soon as the guard opened the barred doors, Belinda flew out. *I'm free. This is so wonderful. Now where do I begin? Ah yes. I must see Daisy                                                                    again.*

# Chapter 2
## Belinda and Daisy

Belinda calls out. "Oh Daisy."

"Is that you Belinda? How did you get out of prison?

"I used my spell to have the guard do my bidding."

"Get out of here!"

"That isn't the way to treat me Daisy."

Belinda suddenly points her wand at Daisy and issues the spell. "ZALUMA!" Daisy was overcome by Belinda and her evil curse. "Ah, that is much better. Welcome back Daisy."

"Thank you. So, what brings you out here?

"I am back for revenge on Eric Thompson."

"Why?"

"He overcame me and I need to exact my revenge."

"How will you do that?"

"That is where you come in."

"Me? How?"

"Well this is what I want you to do. Call him and find out where he is."

"What will you do?"

"I will go to his house and get all his things."

"That is a great idea, Belinda. I'll give him a call."

# Chapter 3
# Eric

*Hours before Belinda came…*

"It is so great to be home," said Eric. "That was a tough battle with Belinda. I'm happy she's gone. legendary hero?

"Yes, Eric?"

"Can you come over here for a minute?"

"Yes. What's up Eric? How are you?"

"I am doing well. Anything new?"

"Nope, everything is at peace."

"Thank you, legendary hero."

"What will you do now Eric?"

"I'm going to work."

"Your Rogue Federal job?"

"Yes."

"Well, have a good one."

"Thank you."

*Present time…*

Ring, Ring, Ring... Eric picked up his phone. "Hello?"

"Hi Eric. This is Daisy."

"Hello Daisy. How are you?"

"I'm doing great. How are you?"

"I'm good. I'm on break. I'll be home around three. Thanks for calling, Daisy. Have a good one."

"You                                                        too."

# Chapter 4
## Belinda's Rampage

Belinda is transported into Eric Thompson's house. *This house looks really good. Eric has everything that he needs here. And no one is even here. This is so good.*

Knock, Knock, Knock. *Now who could that be? Oh, it looks like Daisy has arrived.*

Belinda opens the door. "Welcome to Eric's house, Daisy."

"Thank you. So, what have you done so far?"

"I just arrived."

"I have some good news, Belinda."

"What is that?"

"Eric will not be home until 3:00 pm."

"Excellent. We should have plenty of time before he arrives. What time is it now, Daisy?"

"It is 1:30."

"Wonderful."

"What do you want me to do, Belinda?"

"Well, I would like you to get Eric's things. His books, video games, his life-sized Spiderman and everything else he loves. Even his movies and Blu-ray player. I want him to feel despair when he comes home and finds his things missing."

"I shall do as you ask Belinda. What will you do?"

"I am going to call the house of villains and let them know the plan.

"Good idea, Belinda. I am off." Daisy left and began gathering Eric's things.

The Villains lair was full of villains. They had a big amount. There were villains like hair, blanket, tail, vines, tentacles, sorceresses and last but not least women.

Belinda called the house of villains. Ring, Ring, Ring... "Hello. This is the house of villains."

"Hello my friends. Do you recognize who this is?"

"Yes, Belinda."

"I have some wonderful news. I found Daisy and she's converted to our side."

"That is great news."

"I also am having her get Eric's things. Soon, Eric will be home and he doesn't even know I'm here."

All the villains laughed loudly. "What should we do?"

"Clean up the area and make sure it's spotless, because when Eric gets here he will be on my side."

"You never cease to amaze us, Belinda."

"Why, thank you. See you soon my friends."

As Belinda hung up, Daisy returned. "I did as you asked, Belinda. Everything is in my possession."

"Well-done Daisy. How did you do it?"

"I used my powers to pack everything into an enormous bag, which I have."

"Great. What time is it now?"

"It's 2:30. Eric is home in a half-hour. I am so excited to see him, Belinda."

"So                          am                          I."

# Chapter 5
# Eric Turns Evil

Eric arrived home and saw Daisy's car. He was excited to see her, but little did he know that Belinda was also there. After the battle, he thought that he had stopped her. He was wrong. What Eric hadn't realized was that the biggest battle was over, but the war was not yet won. He went into his room and noticed something strange. *My goodness! What happened? Who was responsible for this?* His phone was gone, his books. He checked upstairs. To his dismay the TV was gone. He went downstairs to the family room. His Eye TV was gone too. He checked inside the closet door. The video games were gone. Eric went back to his room and hung his head in disappointment. *Who could have done this? If Belinda was free, she might have done it.* I can't be sure if she was even here.

Daisy knocks on the door. "Eric?"

"Who is this?"

"Daisy. May I come in?"

"Sure."

Daisy opens the door.

"Hi, Daisy."

"What's the problem Eric?"

"It seems that someone has taken all my stuff away."

"Who could have done that?"

"I don't know. What am I supposed to do?"

"You just need to find the person who did it and then convince them to return everything to you."

"That doesn't help me, Daisy." Eric walked into another room and Daisy followed.

Standing in the room was Belinda. A look of surprise came on Eric's face. "Belinda. How did you get out of prison? Oh, I know how you got out!"

"How do you think I got out, Eric?"

"You must have had your wand hidden with you in the cell. You used your bidding spell and made the guard open the bars."

"How did you know, Eric?"

"It wasn't hard to figure out. I had a feeling that you were free, even though I didn't know it for sure."

Belinda admitted the theft. "It was I who stole your things. I didn't do it by myself. I had Daisy do it."

"Daisy, you are my friend." Why?"

Daisy looked directly at Eric. "That is where you are wrong, Eric. I am a sorceress. Belinda overcame me and she made me like this. This is how I really look."

Belinda points her wand at Eric. "Now you will see how long I have been waiting to get my revenge on you. I'm not going to harm you. No. I'm going to make you evil like me. Where is your legendary hero now when you need him?" Belinda shouts, "ZALUMA."

Eric dodged Belinda's spell, but could not dodge Daisy, the sorceress, who stopped him with her powers and held him in place until Belinda said "ZALUMA" again causing Eric to become evil like Belinda and Daisy.

# Chapter 6
# Nicholas Parker

Nicholas!! Nicholas. Come Quick!!

Nicholas came inside the door.

He kneeled. My king!

We have a serious issue on our hands!!

And what would it be?

Eric Thompson has turned evil!

Nicholas looked at him perplexed.

Eric? I don't think I know him.

But he knows you. In fact, he thinks highly of you.

Really?

Really!

So how do you know about this?

The Legendary Hero gave me a computer so I could watch everything that's happening.

The Legendary Hero? Who's he? Maybe another dimension?

You got that right. He's the one who discovered the threat alert in his lab.

And he's turning to you?

No. He's trusting **You** Nicholas. He hopes that you can secretly see what he's doing and then find the legendary Hero. The computer can transport you instantly to any location.

It can? What about David? Should he come too?

No!! He'll be seen. You have been entrusted to this task. After all, you're stealthy and you're good at not being seen.

Then it is my responsibility! I will go!

Oh. And Nicholas?

Yes?

Be Careful!!
Where am I going?
Eric was last seen in a church building. You must go to Medford City Hall.
I Give you my word!! Computer!!
Yes?
Take me to Medford City Hall
Beginning transportation.

# Chapter 7
## Eric, Daisy and Belinda Reunite

Belinda watched as Eric went through the transformation. "How are you doing, Eric?"

"I'm doing very well, thank you, Belinda. How are you Daisy?"

"I am doing well, Eric. Thank you."

"So, what brings you here, to my house, Belinda?"

"Well, I thought maybe it would be a good idea to bring your stuff to the house of villains and have them enjoy it."

"That's just fine with me. What do you want to do, Belinda?"

"Well it's all up to you. After all, you know where to go and I don't."

"Well-said, Belinda."

"What should I do?" asked Daisy.

Belinda answered, "Well, you can go anywhere you want. Does that sound good, Eric?"

"Okay with me."

"Where will you and Belinda go?"

"We will go to City Hall where I used to go."

"That's an excellent choice Eric," said Belinda.

Eric looked over at Daisy. "Actually, Daisy, there is something you can do for me."

"What is that?"

"You can bring my stuff to the house of villains and set it all up there. Let them know I said hi."

"Will do, Eric."

"What about Rone and Crystal, Eric?" Daisy asked."

"Leave them alone. They don't need to interfere with our plans. There is no need to capture anybody. We're all just there to have a good time."

"Ok, then, Belinda. It has been decided. We will go to the singles ward first."

"Where else will we go, Eric?"

"After the singles ward, we'll go to Medford City Hall, and then to the land of Ashello, and last to the House of Villains."

"Great           plan           Eric.           Let's           go."

# Chapter 8
# Daisy's Preparation at the House of Villains

There was a knock on the door of the House of Villains. "Hello? Who is it?"

"It's Daisy the sorceress."

"Hey everybody. Look who's here. It's Daisy. How wonderful."

"Can I come in?"

"Sure, you can." The villains opened the door and let her in. They expressed how happy they were to see her.

"It is so good to see you again, Daisy."

"Thank you."

"How did you know that I had reunited with Belinda?"

"Through our good friend and partner Belinda."

"What's in that big bag you have with you, Daisy?"

"This bag contains everything that Eric Thompson loves."

"All of his stuff?"

"Yes, all of it."

"Now what do we do with it?"

"Well, we need to put it in places where we know we can all play it. Hmmm… you can decide where you want to put it."

"Ok. Sounds great." The villains decided where they wanted to put Eric's things and then the house was prepared.

"Well done my friends. Now. let's get it prepared for Eric and Belinda."

"As you wish, Daisy. What about the heroes?"

"Eric made it clear that we don't need to capture anyone. Just have fun."

"Ok,       then.       We       shall       see       them       soon."

# Chapter 9
## Belinda and Eric's Rampage

"Oh, Eric. It's so nice that we get to do this together."

Eric looks back at Belinda. "I totally agree. It feels good to be bad. Ah, here we are at the building. The singles ward should be inside. Hello? Anybody here?" There was no answer. They entered the building and moved a lot of books from the shelves with the spell power of their wands. They kept this up until the place was a total disaster. They left the mess at the singles ward and flew outside laughing. *What a treat for the singles ward. Wait till they see what's happened.*

Eric and Belinda continued on to the Medford City Hall. They stopped at the police window and Eric said, "Hi."

The personnel behind the window said, "Hi. How is your day Eric?"

"It is awesome."

"Good to hear that. Have a good day Eric."

"Thank you." They went upstairs to the third floor.

Belinda walked into the financial office and said, "Give us your money."

"You have no right."

"Oh, yes we do. Eric? Open that safe."

"With pleasure." With his power, Eric pulled open the safe door and grabbed the money.

One of the people inside the office who knew Eric said, "Eric, I thought you were our friend?"

"I was, but not anymore."

Belinda and Eric went out the door. The phone rang in the police department and was answered by one of the on-duty officers. "Police Department. How can we help you?"

A person, somewhat out of breath said, "Eric and this evil witch have taken money from the finance office."

"Don't worry. We'll take care of it."

As soon as Belinda and Eric got down to the first floor, the police were there with their guns drawn.

The chief said, "Stop, put your hands over your head." Eric and Belinda ran for it.

"Shoot. Shoot." They shot, but Belinda and Eric were out the door. They both waited outside the door.

"Surrender."

"Never," said Belinda.

The chief said, "Eric, why would you do this?"

"Because I'm evil."

"Shoot again." They shot, but this time Eric put out his hands and pushed them out of the way. Little did Eric and Belinda know that there was someone who was recording the whole thing.

Belinda said to Eric, "That was fun, but let's go."

"Okay, hold my hand." They held hands and were transported to Ashello.

# Chapter 10
# The Mysterious Warrior

"I recorded the scene at the City Hall with Belinda and Eric. Where did they come from?" *This is so strange. I thought that Eric was the chosen one.* "Why is he evil?" *I can't believe I ended up in this dimension.* "But how?" *I can only think of one person who did this. The legendary hero.* "Where does Eric live anyway?" *I will go inside City Hall and find out where he came from.*

As he walked into City Hall, he said, "Hello, sir. How are you? I have an issue.'

"We also have an issue."

"What is it?"

"Eric Thompson, our best friend, has turned evil?"

"How is this possible?"

"I don't know, but it sounds as though we have the same issue."

"All I know is that I have a recording of Eric during the scene."

"You do? Let us hear it."

Recording: Eric, why would you do this?"

Because I'm evil. They listened and heard the truth.

The mysterious warrior played the recording again. "I must find Eric. Where does he live?"

"We should have information. Let's take a look." They found papers in the file that described where he lived and told the mysterious warrior.

He left and went to Eric's house. He knocked on the door and the legendary hero opened it.

"Who are you? What are you doing here?"

"I have a message for Eric."

"Do come in mysterious warrior."

"So, you are the legendary hero?"

"Indeed I am."

"I can't say my name in public because they would know my secret identity."

"Who are you?" The mysterious warrior moved the cowl back to reveal his identity as none other than Nicholas Parker.

Nicholas Parker?

"You know my name, legendary hero?"

"Of course, I do. Eric told me all about you. He said that he thinks highly of you."

"I am totally honored legendary hero."

"How did you end up here, Nicholas?"

"Blaze Steven, Princess Charlotte and my best friend David sent me through a portal. They knew something was going to happen. Something fierce. So, they sent me."

"Are they going to come too?"

"Oh, Yes. They are. You just need to send them here."

"How?"

"You have a machine don't you, legendary hero?"

"Yes, I do. Okay then, Nicholas, I shall get them."

While the legendary hero left for the room that housed the machine, Nicholas listened to the recording again. *Why didn't I tell the legendary hero about this? I won't worry. He'll be back.*

# Chapter 11
# Nicholas's Destiny

*Before the legendary hero arrived…*

Charlotte the princess reaches over to shake hands with David. "Oh, David, it is so good to be with you."

"Me too. I have enjoyed everything about Brackinova. Nicholas Parker was the right person to find Eric and that evil witch, Belinda."

"But how did we know?" asked Charlotte?"

"We found out from the King."

"How did he know?"

"He has a way of knowing things. He could see something in the sky. Let's ask him. David."

"Yes. Let's do it."

Charlotte and David got their audience with the king.  David addressed him. "My King."

"Yes, David. What brings you here?

"We wanted to know what you saw from the sky."

"I remember something. As I looked, I saw Eric and an evil witch and they were talking. I had a feeling something terrible would be happening so I called the legendary hero."

"You called him? How? He's in another dimension." Yes. That's true. I remember Nicholas Parker was telling me about the legendary hero. What did he say? He said that the legendary hero lives close to Eric and that he would be the one to tell the legendary hero. So, when he noticed the portal I told him and Samantha to go through it and find the legendary hero. Ok. My king. We shall wait until the legendary hero gets here.

*Present…*

The legendary hero made it to Brackinova. *It is so beautiful.* On approaching the entry gate, he hears a command.

"Halt. Who goes there?"

"I am the legendary hero."

"You, the Legendary Hero?"

"Yes, I am"

"You may enter."

"Who are you?"

"I am Steve, Nicholas Parker's master."

"It is good to meet you Steve. So, what brings you here to Brackinova Legendary Hero?"

"To find Charlotte and David. Do you know where they are?"

"Yes. They are found in the kingdom."

"We have a visitor, David," said Steve.

David asked, "Who might you be sir?"

"I'm the legendary hero."

"You're the Legendary Hero? The most powerful force on earth?"

"Yes. I'm here to take you to Eric's house where your friend Nicholas awaits."

David grinned. "I love an adventure. How do we get there?"

"Grab my hand." David and the legendary hero were transported to Eric's                                                                                     house.

# Chapter 12
# The Truth

David and the legendary hero made it safely through the dimension to Eric's House. On arrival, David greeted his friends, Nicholas and Charlotte.

Nicholas said, "It is so good to see you here David."

"Thanks, Nicholas. What brings you here my friends?"

"We've heard you are on a mission. A dangerous mission. One that if discovered would be the end of the world."

Legendary hero asked, "What's going on Nicholas? Why haven't you told me?"

"I couldn't tell you until the time was right."

"Is it the right time, Nicholas?"

"It is."

"Then tell us."

"I remember the king's words and they were simple. Find Eric and the evil witch, but don't let them see you. Record their whereabouts and then go to Eric's House where the legendary hero is. He will know what must be done. So, go there and don't make yourself known. I have been successful. Eric doesn't even know I'm here."

"Excellent," said David.

The legendary hero's face showed much confusion. "Eric? My apprentice? The chosen one? How can this be? I last talked to him before he went to work, and he was fine. Now, he's turned evil? How can this be? Oh, I remember now. Belinda escaped from jail, found Daisy and then surprised Eric and bound him with her spell "zaluma". He was powerless because he didn't have his wand. He was vulnerable. Where was I when it happened? I was in the lab at Eric Thompson's domain having fun with Frederick, Elphias, and those other good heroes. I came home and this is what I see? I can't believe it."

"Legendary hero, I feel your pain," said Nicholas.

"What must I do?"

"You are the legendary hero and the only one who can stop Eric!"

"I must formulate a plan."

"What ideas do you have," Samantha said.

"We will start by getting all the heroes together to retrieve Eric's things from the house of villains."

"How will we do that?" asked Nicholas.

"The plan is simple. We just need to get the heroes together to battle the villains. While they're battling, and have the villains occupied, I will get Eric under control."

"How can you do that? He's so powerful."

"I'm more powerful than him. Just because I gave him these powers doesn't mean that he will succeed."

"Ok, legendary hero. Let's get the superheroes together."

The legendary hero called the headquarters of the heroes. The phone was answered. "Hello, this is the heroes' headquarters. How can we help you?"

"This is the legendary hero. I have some news my friends."

"You do? What is it?"

"Belinda has turned Eric evil. I'll explain when you get here. Can you come over to my lab?"

"Yes, we can."

"Heroes?"

"Yes, master?"

"We all need to go to Eric's house. Can you come with me?"

"Yes, we can"

"Ok, then, let's get over there." The floors warped and they ended up at Eric's house.

# Chapter 13
# Ashello

Belinda and Eric made it to Ashello and into the prison where Krell was being held.

Eric said, "That was fun Belinda."

"Me too." Belinda began looking for Krell. In a soft voice she said, "Oh, Krell, where are you?"

Krell spoke quietly. "Is that you Belinda?

"Yes. We have come for you." Eric and Belinda walked down the corridor toward the sound of Krell's voice.

"Belinda. It is so good to see you. Eric! What is he doing here?"

Eric answers. "Take it easy, Krell. I'm on your side."

"You are? How can that be?"

Belinda said, "I made him evil, Krell."

"You did? How?"

"I put him under a spell while Daisy held him down. Do you like that?"

"Of course, I do. So, Eric and Belinda. How can you possibly get me out of these bars? You better hurry. I hear Rone and Crystal coming."

Eric and Belinda ran into the darkness and hid. Rone and Crystal didn't know that they were there.

*Before Eric and Belinda arrived…*

Crystal pointed to Krell and looked toward Roan. "Oh, Rone. It's so nice to see Krell behind bars."

"I totally agree with you."

Krell yelled. "Let me out."

"Oh no, Krell, you will not get out."

"Wait till Belinda gets back. Oh, how much danger you will be in."

"Oh, Krell, be serious, Belinda will never rescue you."

"And why not?"

"Because she has been stopped by Eric Thompson."

Krell was left behind bars as Crystal and Rone left.

After a few days, Rone and Crystal returned to where Krell was imprisoned. In the hallway close to his cell, they heard some people talking to Krell. "My goodness, Rone. Who could that be talking to Krell?"

"I don't know. We need to get there fast and find out." They raced to the dungeon.

*Present…*

Rone and Crystal arrived outside Krell's cell, but nobody was there. Rone said, "Whoever was here is gone. I wonder who it was?"

"I don't know." Crystal said. "I feel they are still here." Crystal looked down the hallway. "Where are you? I know you are still here. Show yourself. Krell, who was talking? Tell me."

"Why, no one. I don't know what you are talking about."

Eric and Belinda stayed hidden in the shadows. "I can see Rone and Crystal," whispered Eric.

"Why are they here?" Belinda whispered.

"They are checking on Krell and they don't know we're here."

"What do you want to do Eric?"

"I'm thinking you should confront them."

"Me?"

"Ok. What will you do?"

"You'll see."

"Crystal?"

"Yes, Rone?"

"Do you see anyone?"

"No, I don't."

Belinda walked out from the shadows.

Rone and Crystal were very surprised. Rone said, "Belinda, how did you get out?"

"I still have my powers."

"But, Eric struck you down."

"No, he didn't. He sent me to prison but that didn't stop me. Ha, Ha, Ha."

"Eric. Why are you on Belinda's side?"

"Because I became evil."

"That is not good, Eric." Rone said.

"And why not, Rone?"

"Because you are meant for greatness. Do you remember the time you told me to protect good from evil?"

"I don't remember."

"You can remember, Eric. "Not anymore. What will you do to us?"

"Oh, nothing."

"Nothing? You're not going to lock us in a dungeon?"

"No."

Belinda chimed in. "Eric will not, because we are just having fun. No captures are allowed."

"Was it you saying that or was it Eric?"

"Eric said it."

"Well, that's good. At least there is nothing that will happen to us. Why are you here to see Krell then?"

"We need him."

"Why?"

"Because the villains from the house of villains want him there."

"They do?"

"Krell will never go out," said Rone.

"Oh, and what makes you think you can stop us, Rone?"

"I will defend those bars and you will not be able to touch them."

Belinda raised her wand. "Eric. Free Krell. I'll keep Rone and Crystal away."

Rone looks at Eric. "You can't do this to us. You're our best friend. Snap out of it."

"Never."

While Belinda was keeping Rone and Crystal away from Krell, Eric grabbed hold of the bars and with his powers, yanked them off.

"Eric, you saved me."

"You're welcome, Krell. Now let's get out of here. Come on Belinda. Let's get back to the house of villains."

"After them, Crystal. Don't let them get away." Crystal used her hands and threw her magic at them. The connection broke.

"You can't get away with this, Rone and Crystal."

"Oh yes, we can, Eric. We will not let you get back to the house of villains. It's too dangerous there. You will stay with us. We care about you."

Eric shouts. "Belinda and Krell, get back to the house of villains."

"No, Eric, we won't leave you."

"Go now!"

"Ok, Eric. What will we tell them?"

"Tell them I care about them and will be there very soon."

Belinda told Krell to grab hold of her hand. Krell grabbed her hand and they were transported to the house of villains. Eric continued to be bound on the wall by Crystal's magic.

# Chapter 14
# The House of Villains

Krell and Belinda safely landed in the house of villains.

"Hello everyone. I'm back."

"Belinda, it's so good to see you. Well, Krell, what a pleasant surprise."

"Where's Eric?" Asked the villains.

"Rone and Crystal bound him there."

"What? Are you sure?"

"Yes. We're sure."

"What will we do?"

"There's nothing we can do."

"Are you sure, Belinda?"

"I'm sure."

"I know what we have to do," said one of the villains."

Krell looked at the villain that spoke. "What is your idea?"

"I think that I can bring him back."

"You? Crystal is too powerful. She'll throw you into the wall just like Eric."

"You're right. She will. Forget my idea."

"Who else is powerful here?"

"I am a sorceress."

"You?"

"Let me demonstrate my power."

"Wow. With power like that you may really be able to rescue Eric."

"Yes, I will."

"Ok, then, go get him."

"With pleasure."

Daisy stepped forward. "Oh, Sorceress?"

"Yes?"

"I need to come with you."

"Ok." The sorceress and Daisy are transported to Ashello.

Crystal looked at Rone. "Oh, Rone. I am so happy I stopped Eric from escaping."

Eric looked mean and frustrated. "Let me go Crystal."

"I will not. You are going nowhere. You will stay here until the legendary hero arrives."

"Him? He's more powerful than me."

"Of course, he is."

Just then a sorceress and Daisy land in the dungeon. "Oh, Rone and Crystal, we are here to rescue Eric."

"You really think so?"

The sorceress waved her wand and cast her magic at Crystal and Daisy did the same. While Daisy was busy with Crystal the sorceress blasted Rone out of the way and freed Eric.

"Thanks for saving me, sorceresses. I'm free. Let's get out of here. They stopped blasting Rone and Crystal and transported back to the house of villains.

"No. What have we done? I can't believe we couldn't stop them."

"They were powerful. Don't worry Crystal. We will see them again, and when we do, all the villains will be stopped."

"So, what do we do now, Rone?"

"We wait. The legendary hero will find us and we'll be ready. In the meantime,        let's         practice          our          magic."

# Chapter 15
# The Plan of the Legendary Hero

The legendary hero looked out at the group.

"My friends. It is so good to see all of you again."

Speaking for the group, Nicholas Parker said, "And the same to you, legendary hero. So, why are we here?"

Legendary hero, with your help, do you think we should have a chance to get Eric's things back.

"I do. Absolutely."

"So, what have we missed?"

"Well, everybody. I have some bad news."

"Bad news? How can there be bad news when we're here?"

"Eric has turned evil."

"He's turned evil?"

"Yes, he has."

"What happened?"

"Well, the first thing you need to know is that Belinda escaped from jail. She also put Eric under her spell that turned him evil. I saw him wreak havoc in his church, pushed police officers with his power and broke Krell free in Ashello. He was about to get away when Crystal stopped him and bound him on the wall, but when I looked again he had escaped.

"This is so unexpected," said the superheroes.

"Yes, it is," said Nicholas.

Someone in the group said, "Who is Nicholas Parker?"

He stepped forward. "Hi everyone. I am Nicholas Parker. I'm a protector in a place called Brackinova."

Another person shouted out. "How did you get here?"

"How did I get here? I thought you'd never ask. It all started when I got a message from my king that there was something evil coming to Brackinova. I was transported to this world through a dimension to see what the evil was. It was Eric Thompson. He and Belinda were out there and coming. They didn't even know I was there. They had decided to go to Ashello. That was at the same time I found the legendary hero here at Eric's house."

"So, it's true? You are the chosen one?"

"Yes, I am."

"Thank you for that message, Nicholas."

Standing tall, Nicholas informed the group that it was time to pay a visit to Ashello."

"Why should we go to Ashello?"

"Because, with the help of Rone and Crystal, we can vanquish this evil forever."

"What will you do Legendary Hero?"

"I am going to stop Eric. I can and I will. He needs to get out of his evil self and return to us. Once he is okay, he will be in grave danger. If I were going alone, I wouldn't be able to stop them because they have captured and recaptured him thousands of times. We must get his things back. Are you ready, Nicholas?"

"Yes, I am. Legendary hero?"

"Yes, Nicholas?"

"I want Eric to see me."

"Ok. How are you so sure he will be good again?"

"Because, he will know me and that's when his evil will diminish."

"Are you sure, Nicholas?"

"I'm sure. If he doesn't, then you can stop him from there."

"Ok Nicholas. Let's go to Ashello."

"I hear something Rone. Hide!"

"Rone and Crystal? It's I, the legendary hero."

"Hurray! It's so good to see you. Good to see you all."

"Let's get down to the house of villains and stop them."

"Yes, let's go!"

They were transported to the house of villains.

# Chapter 16
# The Battle

*Before the battle…*

Eric lands in the House of villains!

"I'm back."

"It is so good to see you, Eric. I thought we lost you. What a relief."

"Let's play some of my games."

"Sure." Eric and one of the villains, ivy turned on the TV so everyone could watch movies and play video games. While they played and watched, they heard noises coming from outside. "What was that?"

"I don't know. Let me look." Belinda got up and looked outside.

"Oh, my goodness."

"What is it?"

"All the heroes are gathered outside to get Eric. The legendary hero is out there too."

"Oh no, this isn't good."

Belinda stood in front of the villains. "Everyone will stand their ground. Let them come."

Nicholas stood tall and looked to his right.

"Legendary hero?"

"Yes?"

"Are we going in?"

"Yes, we are. Let's go!" They entered the evil fortress. "Villains, come out wherever you are."

Belinda, followed by most of the villains, came out.

The legendary hero said, "Ah, there they are."

"Belinda shouted. "Villains. Attack.""

Eric, running forward next to Belinda, notices the legendary hero. "Nice of you to drop in."

"Eric, this is madness."

"Of course, it is."

"I brought a couple of people with me that you might want to see," said the legendary hero.

"And who might that be?

"Samantha, David, and Nicholas, stepped out."

Eric's face was concerned. "Nicholas, David, Samantha, what are you doing here?"

"We are here to see you."

"See me?"

"Of course. We need you to be good again."

"How can I be good? I'm evil. I'm still under Belinda's spell."

Nicholas said, "Eric, I know that there is some good in you."

"Why can't you believe in yourself? Eric! you can return to normal. I will see to it that you become good again."

"Are you sure Nicholas?"

"I'm sure."

Eric saw that his evil had caused a lot of damage. He thought back to his times with the singles ward and his memory returned. As the fighting between the villains and the heroes continued, Eric got his mind clear and was good again.

The legendary hero spoke up loudly. "Eric, we need to get out of here." He gave Eric his wand.

Belinda yelled. "Eric, where are you going?"

"I am no longer under your spell, Belinda."

Belinda said "**ZALUMA**" and Eric said "**STRASINKO**." The spells collided and then the connection broke.

"You will come back with me Eric."

"That is where you are wrong, Belinda."

"Let's get out of here."

"As you wish, said the legendary hero." With a flick of his wand Eric said, "**cray**" which got Eric's things in a bag. They were transported home.

# Chapter 17
# The Adventure Ends

*After the battle…*

Eric's things were back in his home safe and sound.

"Nicholas, David, and Samantha?"

"Yes, Eric?"

"Thank you for helping me understand myself. I don't know how I would've gotten out of Belinda's spell without your help. She returned and I was vulnerable. Now she's gone. I'm relieved. There were so many things on her mind. My friends would be shocked to know that the church was demolished. But, I can fix everything. Oh, yes I can."

"You're welcome Eric. What will you do now?"

"Now? Well the world is at peace. I'll go to Medford City Hall, the singles ward, and home. Farewell my friends."

# Chapter 18
## Eric Makes Things Right

*Eric got to Medford City Hall and opened the door.*
*He went to the third floor, the financial office.*

Eric? What are you doing here? I'm here to return the money that the evil witch and I took. Here's your money back."

"Why were you evil?"

"Belinda, the witch, had a spell that made me do her bidding. It was called Zaluma. I am happy that I'm back to normal. I'm sorry that I stole the money. I'm going to talk with the police department now."

"Hello? Yes sir? How can we help you?" the police supervisor said.

"I'd like to say sorry."

"For what?"

"Earlier today an evil witch and I stole some money. Do you remember now?"

"Oh yeah. That's right. Why would you do that? I was under the witch's evil spell. I'm back to normal."

"Thank you for telling us, Eric. I hope you have a good day."

"Thanks. Same to you."

*Eric arrived at the singles ward.*

"Hello? Anybody here?"

"A man was walking around and opened the door."

"What are you doing here? Don't you know that this building is locked and messy here?"

"No. I didn't know."

"Then get out of here."

"No. I can't."

"Why not?"

"Because I need to fix things here."

"You do? Why was this building messed up?"

"An evil witch and I were responsible for this mess. I'm here to restore peace in this church. I'm sorry. Can I come in?"

"Yes. You can.'

"Hmmm…. What can I do to get this church clean again? Ah. I do have something."

"You have a wand?"

"Of course. Watch this."

The man watched in amazement as Eric used his powers to get everything clean. When Eric was done he removed his hood.

"Eric ! I'm surprised "You are a good man Eric. Thank you for cleaning this church. It means a lot to me and the ward.

"You're very welcome. I am going to go home now."

"Ok Eric. I wish you well."

"You                              too                              bishop."

# Chapter 19
# Eric returns Home

"Legendary hero?

"Yes, Eric?"

"I'm back."

"Welcome home, my friend. It's good to have you back. I wish you the best, Eric."

"Thank you, legendary hero."

So, after the adventure, Eric went into his room and rested.

# Epilogue

As peace returned Braille and Sheryl were side by side in Trista. Their twins were born.

It's time. Said Sheryl.

It is time dear.

We have a new chapter in our lives. We have children. And soon we will see Eric again.

Yes. We will Braille. In this dark time there is light.

Hang in there Eric!! I'll be back soon.

Just hold on a little longer.

Do you think Eric will be ready to face Malcolm? Said Sheryl.

There's no doubt in my mind that he will. I'm sure he's grown more powerful. And even if he did get captured he is likely to be rescued. After all, he has many superheroes around him for support. There's no doubt in my mind that he will train our children well.

And I know we will stop Braze once and for all.

## The End of Part 3

# Part 4 – Rise of a Family

By Eric Thompson

*Introduction*

Previously there was peace. Suddenly a dark force appears that Eric doesn't expect in addition to Belinda's return. Eric Thompson trains a family to defeat powerful enemies.

# Chapter 1
# A Dark Force Emerges

Matt said, "Ah, isn't it great that we're together?"

"Yes. It is," said Amber.

The family were playing games and watching tv.

"What did you think of the movie?" Fred said.

"I thought it was great," said Mary. "I haven't seen Eric Thompson for a while."

"Neither have we," said Dash. "Whaddaya say we invite him over."

"That's a great idea," Claire said.

Suddenly out of the shadows, a dark lord entered the house without knocking. "Well, hello there. I'm here to steal some things from you."

Matt stepped forward and said, "You have NO RIGHT!"

"Oh yes I do." He then said, "**Bracio**". A spell that pushes people away. When one person tried to push him back, he said "**Kelo**" which is a stunning spell.

Ben yelled, "Stop Him!" Try as they might, they couldn't stop him. He flung his cape to avoid them. "Your stuff is mine now. You will never have it back." Using his dark powers, he tied up everybody and then grabbed all their things. "Ha, ha, ha! Victory is mine!" After he left, the darkness disappeared and the family was untied.

Ben said, "Mom? Dad? Oh no. Our things are gone. How can this be?"

Max answered. "Well we do know one thing. We know that he has dark powers and that we cannot stop him."

"I wish we had powers," Ben said.

"Yes. We need someone who could grant us powers. But who?" Matt said.

"I might know someone," Amber said. "He talks about his books a lot. More and more I'm convinced that he might be the one who could stop the dark lord."

"Who?" Claire said.

"Why, Eric Thompson."

"Eric Thompson? Hmm. I think I've heard about him. He has many accomplishments. How can we reach him? I don't know his number."

"That could be a problem. But, I think there is a way to reach him."

"Let's consider our options," Fred said. "First, we know he has a lot of books he's written and second, we know that the legendary hero is in some of his stories.

"That's it. The legendary hero will tell Eric about us. But how can we reach the legendary Hero? Oh well. I guess we'll find out.

*Meanwhile, with the legendary hero in his home.*

"Man alive. I can't figure out how to make this dessert for Eric. This is ridiculous. How am I supposed to make something if I don't know how to do it?"

"Eric would know."

"After all the times I've helped him, by now, I should know enough to make this dessert.

"That's ok. I don't need to work on this right now."

Beep, beep, beep… "Seems, I have a message from the computer."

"Computer?"

"Yes, legendary hero."

"I just received a message for you."

"What is it?"

"On the TV there's a family asking for help. Play the video."

"As you wish."

The video stated the family's needs. "We need to stop the evil dark lord. We know that Eric can help. Where can we find him?"

"Ah! Just as I suspected. Thanks computer. I shall find Eric now.

Ring, ring, ring…. "Hello? This is Eric Thompson."

"Hello Eric."

"Legendary Hero?"

"Yep. It's me. What's up?"

"Well Eric, there's a family who needs your help."

"They need my help? Do you know where they are?"

"Of course."

Demetrius said, "Computer."

"Yes?"

"Track the location of the family."

The computer responds.. Ah. Here they are.  Do you want me to transport you?

"No thanks."

Eric put the address in his phone and went over there.

*Eric drove over.*

# Chapter 2
# Family Receives Powers

Eric arrives. "So, this is the family that wants to have powers? What kind of powers do they want?"

"Well, I know that Malcolm, the dark lord, is wreaking havoc somewhere. But where?"

"I'm not sure."

"I'll find him somewhere. In the meantime, I will visit this family."

Eric went to the house and knocked on the door. As the door opened, Eric said, "Hi. I'm Eric Thompson."

"Eric Thompson? You must be the one who can help us stop the dark lord."

"Yes. That's right. Tell me what happened."

"Ok," Linda said.

"We were having fun playing games and watching TV when a dark figure appeared outside our front door. He didn't even knock, just came inside. He cast a spell that immediately tied us up. From there his spell cast a darkness over us. When he left we were all of a sudden unbound. We don't know where he went. But, when we looked around, all of our things were gone."

"Oh my. Just like that?"

"Yes."

"So, you need powers?"

"Yes. We do."

Matt stepped forward. "I want the power of strength."

Eric transferred this power to Matt.

Claire stepped forward. "I want the power of invisibility."

"Granted."

Max stepped forward.

"What do you want for your power?" Eric asked.

"I want to be a sorcerer."

"You shall receive that power."

Dash stepped forward. "I want the power of speed."

"Mary stepped forward. "I want the power to read minds."

"You have it.

Amber stepped forward. "I want the ability to fly."

"Fly?"

"Yes."

"Ok. You shall have it."

Ben stepped forward. "I want to be a ninja."

"You shall become one."

"Eric, there's two more girls," Claire said.."

"Ok. What powers should they have?"

"I'm not sure. What do you think, Eric?"

"Hmmm... Annabelle will become hot to the touch. Linda will have the power to shoot red hot arrows."

"Wow. I love those powers. Can you train us?"

"Of course. There is a place where we should go to train."

"Where is that?"

"It's in another dimension, called Eric's Domain."

"Ok. Let's go."

"But, we'll need to go to my house first.

*They went to Eric's House.*

# Chapter 3
# Eric's New Spell

"Wow, Eric. We made it," Mary said.

"You have a great house. Do you like to live here Eric?" Max asked.

"Yes, I do. I also make meals every so often."

"You do?" Claire said. "Yep, let's continue on."

Yes. Let's. Hmm...

What is it Eric said Claire?

You all need wands!

Wands?

Yes. Without wands you can't transport to my domain. Hmm... let's see here. Perhaps I should use a spell that can multiply wands here. I'm not sure how to do that.

"That is a problem, said Max.

It is. But I'm sure I can figure it out. In the meantime help yourself to anything in the fridge.

Eric thought hard about the duplication spell.

I remember Meesto is a slowing down spell so that won't work. Let's see here. Eric spoke the incantation "Cust" (coost) which broke something. Nope. Not that one.

Everything ok in there Eric?

Nope!! Just tried a spell that didn't work!

Good luck!!

Thanks! Ok. Let's try this one more time. He spoke the incantation very clearly "estumega"

It was a success.

Yes. I got us all wands!!

Mission Accomplished!!

You got more wands??

Everyone was fascinated by the number of wands.

How did you do it?

Just spoke an incantation and it worked the second time just like I knew it would.

How do we use a wand?

It's pretty simple. Say Strasinko!

Strasinko!

Well done!! That's the attacking spell.

Now to transport, say Porifay.

Now imagine clearly where you want to go with the location. You have to say Porifay first. Ok?Wands at the ready.

Porifay to Eric's Domain

*Porifay to Eric's Domain!!*

*The family and Eric transported to Eric's Domain*

"Ah, we have arrived," said Eric. Waiting in a group was Frederick, the legendary hero, Frederick , and Elphias who said, "Is that Eric I see?"

"Yes, it is. Hello my friends."

"Who are these people?" Frederick asked."

"They are a family that I've granted certain powers to."

"That's awesome," Frederick said.

"But why the powers?" Elphias said.

Eric answered. "Because Malcolm, an evil dark lord, stole all of their things from their home."

"He did?" The legendary hero said.

"Yes, and something needs to be done," Max said.

"Yes," Claire said.

"What can we do?" Linda said.

Eric responded. "Well, first, I need to find Malcolm."

"You?" Matt said. "You'll get captured."

"Not necessarily. I just need to be in the air where they won't see me."

"But what if you get spotted?"

"I'll fly away... Wait a minute! I have an idea."

"What is it?" Matt asked.

Eric continued. "Will Claire step forward?"

Claire, somewhat puzzled, looks at Eric. "Me?"

"Yes."

"What do you want me to do?"

"You have the power of invisibility so you can listen to what the dark lord has to say without being seen."

"That's a brilliant idea," Elphias said.

"So how do I get close enough to hear him? I can't fly."

"You're right. But, maybe I can get you close enough without either of us being seen. So that you can listen to the dark lord's plan and then I'll fly you back."

"Sounds awesome, Eric. Let's find Malcolm."

Eric reached out to Claire. "Hold my hand."

*Off Eric and Claire went to search for Malcolm, the evil dark lord.*

# Chapter 4
## Malcolm's Plan

*Eric circled in the sky until he could find Malcolm.*

"Ah. There he is," said Eric, as he looked at Claire. "Are you ready?"

"Yes. I am."

"Ok. Remember, you need to be as quiet as possible."

"I will." Claire quietly spoke the command and went invisible. She then moved closer to Malcolm. She stopped at a point that was close enough to hear him.

A number of the villains were gathered to listen to Malcolm. "My friends," Malcolm said loud enough for everyone to hear. "This is a good time to take back what's ours. As you recall, Eric escaped from you and Belinda was sent away. Well, she's back and is in Medford right now helping us with our plan. She's contriving lots of traps to capture Eric and his friends. Once she has laid these traps, my plan to take over the world will be executed."

The villains cheered. One of them asked, "So what do we do now?"

"Using one of Belinda's traps set at the superheroes training grounds, we capture Eric and his friends."

"You sure?"

"Yes."

Claire sent a message to Eric. "I have a plan. We must get out of here before they see us."

"Ok. I'll swing on over. Let's go."

Malcolm had the villains all excited. "Are you ready to capture Eric and his friends?"

"Yes. We are. Let's get them." This was the last thing Claire heard as Eric grabbed her hand.

*Eric and Claire flew as fast as they could back to Eric's Domain.*

# Chapter 5
# The Rescue of the Family

*As Eric flew back to Eric's Domain there was evil on the horizon.*

"Oh my gosh, Claire, the villains have captured your family."
"How did they get there before us?"
"Oh, I know. They must have been transported."
"What will we do, Eric?"
"We need to stop them. But, only I am powerful enough to do that."
"What do you want me to do?"
"Claire, keep yourself invisible."
"Ok. But, what about you?"
"I'll change into Batman"
"Batman? You can change into any superhero?"
"Yes, I can."
"They wouldn't be able to tell if it's me."
"Ok. Let's do this.
Villains said, "Look! Up in the sky. It's Batman. We already have a Batman. There's another Batman? I didn't know there could be two. "He's coming in. Look out Malcolm." "Aaaaahhhh! "Don't hurt me," Malcolm said as Batman landed.
"Let go of the family. NOW!"
"Whatever you say Batman. Where is Eric?"
"I don't know where he is."
There's got to be a reason he disappeared!!
Beats me.
When will he show up?
Maybe he will. Maybe he won't.
Eric!! I know you're there. Come out wherever you are.
Eric took off the costume.

You're looking for me?! Here I am.

"Claire, get your family into the portal." Eric said. "I'll hold off Malcolm." "**STRASINKO**." Malcolm got blasted back. "NOOOOO!!!! You won't get away with this. Malcolm said. *"This isn't over Eric!"*

"No Malcolm. It's only the beginning.

*Eric and the family escaped through the portal.*

# Chapter 6
## Malcolm's Frustration

Malcolm was very upset. "Aaaahhh! We almost had them. I had the best villains to capture Eric. How did he know about me? He must've been eavesdropping while I was carrying out the plan.

You are quite correct my lord.

I can't believe that Eric escaped me.

Computer? Tell me your secrets."

The computer asked. "Password?"

Malcolm replied, "I don't have a password." Malcolm in his most forceful voice commanded, "COMPUTER, TELL ME YOUR SECRETS."

The computer repeated the question. "Password?"

To which Malcolm repeated. "PASSWORD?" Now Malcolm was really getting aggravated.

"Why won't it tell me about Eric's Domain? Okay, that's it. I'm getting rid of everything.

*Malcolm started destroying everything.*

# Chapter 7
# Belinda Returns

Belinda is very pleased with herself. "Ah. It's so nice to be back in Medford. So many things that I enjoy helping my brother with. These traps will be perfect for Eric and his friends. I can't wait to see him. Boy will he be shocked."

*Meanwhile back at Eric's home.*
"Ah, we made it. That was so close Eric. I can't believe that my family and I were almost captured. I'm happy I eavesdropped. If I hadn't we all would've been captured.
Thank you so much Eric.
You're welcome Claire.
    "Eric, how did you change into Batman?"
    "The legendary hero received those powers long ago and he passed them to me."
    "That's awesome. So, what now," asked linda
    Eric thought for a minute. "We need to train. But before that, we need to understand something."
    "What is that?"
    "Malcolm, the dark lord, has a plan. Claire overheard it and told me."
    "The legendary hero asked, "was she close enough to hear the details?"
    "Yes, she had her invisibility turned on and she was very close. Claire, repeat what you told me about the plan."
    Claire looks directly at Eric for encouragement. She began. "The dark lord's plan is to take over the world. His first step was to capture us. His sister, Belinda, is somewhere. She set traps all over that will help her brother succeed in his plan."
    Eric nods his head. "Belinda is nearby. But, I'll stop her."

"You?" Frederick said.

"Yes, my friend." Eric slaps him on the back. "She's more powerful than ever. But, I'll be able to stop her. I've stopped her before."

"What if you got captured?" Matt asked.

"Then you would have to be the one to rescue me."

"Ok. It's settled then."

"Be careful Eric." Mary said."

"Thank you."

*Eric heads out to find Belinda.*

Eric communicates. "Belinda, show yourself. Where are you?"

"Ah. Eric. There you are. It's nice to see you again. I'm not evil anymore." Eric said.

"Oh, you're not?

"Nope."

"I don't believe it."

"Well, that is unfortunate. I'm ready to capture your friends. I've become more powerful than ever.

Belinda shouts. "**Mela "STRASINKO"**.

"Whoaaa! Cords!" Eric said.

"Oh yes, Eric. Witness my rise to power."

As the cords swarmed toward Eric he jumped out of the way. He cast the spell again but it had no effect on the cords. It was no use. The cords wrapped around him and he dropped his wand.

Ha Ha!! Got you!!

Let me go Belinda!!

You're not going anywhere!! You're going back to my brother Malcolm and in the clutches of the villains. You were lucky last time. This time you're powerless. Where is the legendary Hero and Spider-Man when you need them? Ha Ha Ha

# Chapter 8
## A Disturbance

Claire!! Come quick!!

What is it Legendary Hero?

Eric has been captured!! Again!!

Again? You mean he was captured before?

Correct.

How can we train without him?

That is a problem. If you can't be trained how will you use your powers to rescue him?

You bring a good point; Legendary Hero.

Something must be done in order to rescue him but what? Let's consider the options. It's me, Spider-Man, Elphias the wizard, Frederick the swordsman, Rone, Crystal and last but not least David and Nicholas Parker the archer. We all have a variety of heroes. Some to rescue Eric and some to train you. Let's have a meeting to discuss what we should do.

That's a good idea!! Let's do it.

I'm going to gather the heroes together. Watch this!! Computer!!

Yes??

Find all the superheroes and have them call me.

Yes.

Ring…..

Hello? This is the Superhero headquarters. This is Batman. How can I help?

Hey Batman. This is the Legendary Hero. Eric has been captured again.

This isn't good. I'll send a message out.

Thank you.

Attention All Superheroes. We need to meet in Eric's Domain for an important meeting. Who's with me?

We're coming.

We've all been called here for a reason. And that reason is not only to rescue Eric but to train this family of powers.

This is intriguing. What are their powers? What should be done about Eric? For one thing we need to get him back.

I have an idea!

What's your idea; Legendary Hero?

My idea is to send Rone Crystal Nicholas and David.

That's a great idea! We think that you should train the family. After all, You're the most powerful superhero in the world!!

Then it's settled!! I'll train the family and the four heroes will rescue Eric. Thank you for all your help again!!

It was our pleasure!!

## Chapter 9 Belinda and Malcolm

Hmmmfff!!

Belinda had a handkerchief over Eric's mouth. Eric tried to move but he was bound from his mouth to his hands. Belinda made it back to her brother's lair. The villains were sitting down and enjoying themselves.

Oh Villains!! Look who I got!!

It's Eric!! It's so good to see him again. All tied up. Ha ha.

Well done Belinda!!

Thank you brother. What have you been doing?

I was just destroying Eric's Domain. I wasn't very happy that he escaped but I'm happy you've brought him to me.

You're welcome.

He was eavesdropping when he heard about my plan.

Well that was unfortunate since I've captured him.

So what should we do with Eric?

What do you think Malcolm?

It's your choice Belinda.

Villains?

Yes Belinda?

Have fun with Eric. He's all yours.

Yes. We shall. Come here Eric.

Eric had nowhere to go.

The tail villain, hair villain and blanket villain wrapped around him.

We love to see you struggle. Ha ha ha.

They took him into their room.

We shall have so much fun with Eric in our hands. Let's get his stuff.

Have a good time, said Daisy.

Thank you Daisy. Eric won't ever escape.


The villains were all happy with glee and they went to bed. Before they went to sleep the women decided to get Eric from the villain's room. They gladly let the women grab him and they tied up his hands and feet so he wouldn't escape.

Sleep well Eric!!

Wait till my friends arrive to rescue me. You'll be in trouble then!!

Oh hush up as they put a handkerchief over his mouth.

Belinda and Daisy peered in.

Goodnight ladies. Have a good time with Eric! Sleep well. Looks like he's all snug. Ha ha ha.

As Eric lay there all bound he thought "Where are you guys?" "Get me out of here!"


*Meanwhile while Eric was bound.....*


Hang in there Eric. Your friends are on their way to rescue you said Spider-Man.

Spider-Man decided to find where he was.

Computer?

Yes?

Find where the house of villains is.

Found it.
So that's where he is.
Spider-Man called the Legendary Hero.
Ring… hello? This is the Legendary Hero!!
Hi.
Spider-Man! What's up?
I found where Eric is.
Where is he?
The villains lair. I'm going to go there.
Don't go Spidey. You'll be captured.
I won't be captured! I'm just going to have a closer look to see where
Eric is being held.
Ok. Be careful.
I promise.
Take care of the family while I'm gone. I'm going to find Rone Crystal
David and Nicholas. They will be the ones to rescue Eric. I'll meet you
at the final battle with Belinda's brother Malcolm.
I give you my word. I'll train the family. Farewell Spider-Man.

# Chapter 10
# The Legendary Hero explains the plan

Claire and her family were awaiting Eric's return from Belinda.

I'm surprised, said Mary. He'd be back by now.

Maybe he got captured, said Max.

You're quite right about that Max. He is captured.

Legendary Hero!! You're here!

I am.

So what should be done? Said Amber?

Well. For one thing, said the legendary Hero, we do need to rescue him. I know who will rescue him.

Who? Said everyone in unison.

Not one person. Four people. I will train you to become the heroes you need to become.

That's wonderful, said Claire. We have a pretty good idea how to use our powers. I remember going invisible when I was listening to Malcolm's plan.

That's a really good power Claire.

Thank you Legendary Hero.

You're welcome.

So where do we start Legendary Hero?

We start at Ashello.

Where is Ashello?

I'll show you. Follow me.

They followed him to a lab.

Wow!! This is an awesome place! The family said.

It is!! It has everything.

Such as? Said Linda

Such as a computer, threat detector, transportation device, weapons etc..

So this is how we go anywhere, said Matt.

You are right Matt!! It is. Now everyone. Stand on the platform! One last thing before we go. My real name is Demetrius.

Sounds great, Demetrius.

Computer!

Yes?

Take us to Ashello!!

Beginning transportation.

# Chapter 11 The Training Begins

"Wow. We're in a different land." Claire said.

"Yes, we are. This will give you a lot of space to train." "Yes. This is a big space."

Where are we? Said max

We are in Ashello!

Before we begin I want to know all your powers.

We'd love to.

I'm Claire. My ability is invisibility

I'm Matt. My ability is strength

I'm Max. I have the powers of a sorcerer.

I'm Amber. I can fly

I'm Mary. I have the power of persuasion

I'm Linda. I have the ability to shoot a fire arrow.

I'm Ben. I can become a ninja.

And this is our baby girl Annabelle. Whoever touches her will have extreme pain from heat.

You all have great powers! Powers that you can use to help other people.

Spider-Man has that philosophy for himself.

That's fascinating, said Amber.

Are you all ready to train?

We are!!

Let's start with you Matt!!

"Matt?"

"Yes, Demetrius ?

"I want you to hit me as hard as you can. Can you do that?"

"You want me to hit you as hard as I can?"

"Of course. You have incredible strength which you can use against your enemies."

"Ok. I'm going for it." Matt hit him hard. He went down and got back up.

"Well done Matt. Computer?"

"Yes?"

"I want you to send the enemy." They advanced toward Matt and he knocked each one out.

"Well done, Matt."

"Thank you."

"Claire. You're next."

"Ok, Demetrius ."

Demetrius looked at Claire. "With your invisibility you can foil an enemy. You may not have what it takes to fight in the battlefield but you can turn off the enemy's source of power."

"That's brilliant."

"Mary?"

"Yes?"

"Since you have the power to read minds you can force the enemy to fight each other."

"Awesome."

"Amber?"

"Yes, Demetrius m?"

"You have the power to fly, which is totally awesome. You have strength as well. You can pound the ground with your punch which will scatter the enemy. Now here's your lesson. Follow me into the air." Into the air they flew. "Computer?"

"Yes, Demetrius ?"

"Send the enemy onto the ground."

"Done." The enemy began to appear on the ground.

"Ok, Amber. Are you ready?"

"Yes, I am."

"Good. You take that side and I'll take the other. On the count of three. One, two, three..." They flew down and each of the enemy was knocked out. "Well done Amber."

"Linda?"

"Yes, Demetrius?"

Have you ever shot targets with your arrows?

Not that I recall.

"You have the power to shoot fire arrows. You always have a target to shoot at. Hold the bow like this and sight your target. Pull back and release. There you go. You're doing very well." Linda. I'm going to do a virtual simulation.

What's a virtual simulation?

You'll have an opportunity to fight an enemy that I ask the computer to send.

Will it hurt me?

Of course not. It's not real. The battle will be real but this isn't real. All you have to do is shoot the enemy just like you did with the targets. Are you ready?

Yes! Send an enemy!

You heard her Computer. Send an enemy."

The enemy appeared.

"Get ready, Linda. Ready. Aim. Fire.

The arrow struck home. "

Great job. Well done!!

"Annabelle is the baby of course. If one of the enemy, or even Malcolm, touched her, their hand would burn."

"Max. You can easily take on Malcolm. He may have experience but you'd be a good match for him. Prepare yourself. Computer? Send Malcolm."

"Malcolm? Ok." The dark lord came after Max. He dodged out of the way and pinned Malcolm to the wall with his powers.

"Well done, Max."

"Thanks, Demetrius ."

 Dash?"

"I want you to run as fast as you can."

Demetrius instantly turned himself into the flash.

"Flash," said Dash. "This is awesome."

"You ready, Dash?"

"Yes I am."

"Get ready. GO." They zoomed around the field. "Good job Dash."

"Hi, Ben."

"Hi, Demetrius."

"You have the power of a ninja. Just like Batman, you have the ability to use your ninja skills. Let's see."

Ben demonstrated his ninja skills.

"Great. With skills like that you can defeat anyone. Computer?"

"Yes?"

"Send a ninja." Ben got in a defensive position and started punching the ninja. He flipped over the ninja and then knocked him out.

"Great job, Ben. You're all ready for the battle."

They all offered a thank you to Demetrius for training them.

*Suddenly in the distance, Rone and Crystal rode a horse to see what was going on.*

"Rone. There's a bunch of people fighting in the field. I'm surprised that they're here. Why would they be here?"

"I don't know, Crystal. Maybe Eric is here training them."

"Hey, everybody. I see two people in the distance and they're coming this way. What should we do?" Max said.

"Demetrius answered, "don't fear, just be patient. If they're bad, I'll take them on."

*Rone and Crystal arrived.*

"Legendary Hero?"

"Yes, it's me."

"Who are these people?" Crystal asked.

"They're all a family who have been given special powers."

"What kind of powers do they have?"

"Power of invisibility, strength, shooting fire arrows, ninja skills, flying, swordsman, reading minds, speed, and this baby can burn anyone who touches her."

"That's totally amazing."

"It is Rone."

"So why are you training here?"

The Legendary Hero explained about Malcolm and Eric's capture.

"Oh my. That's bad, Legendary Hero."

You can call me Demetrius.

Demetrius?

Yes, Crystal.

This is a major problem. With Eric being captured again we need to rescue him.

You both can't do it alone. They'll capture you too. But there are two other people who need to come as well.

Who?

Nicholas and David.

The ones from the other dimension?

Yes. Without them you can't succeed by yourselves.

How can we get them over here? We don't know how to get into a dimension.

All we know is how to transport.

It's the same thing. All you need to do is say the location you want. "Brackinova!"

That makes sense. I think there's one person who should be on our side.

Krell!

Are you nuts Crystal? He'll capture us again. You really think he can change his ways?

I have a feeling it should work. After all, he should have some good in him.

Well said Crystal.

Thank you Demetrius.

Before you go I'm thinking that if you and Crystal are interested you can live with the legendary hero and the warriors he trained."

"Are you serious? Of course, we would love to. "Well, I know we've stopped Krell. But, if we leave Ashello, he might take over the land."

"That's true. But, maybe there might be a way for me to turn him into a good person."

Everybody said, "how?"

"Well, "Once I've convinced Krell to be good, Belinda just might follow and let Eric go. It's worth a shot. Evil can be turned into good. I know that for a fact."

"Ok. It's settled then. I'll keep training the family and you find David and Nicholas

"Ok. Let's go see Krell." With Krell on our side we just might be able to rescue Eric after all.

# Chapter 12
## Krell

"Legendary Hero, Rone and Crystal. What are you doing here? Capturing me again?" Krell said.

"No."

"What are you doing here then?

We're not here to fight you. Rather, we're here to help you. Said Rone.

"Give me a reason why I shouldn't capture you. Right Now!!

"Because you are meant for something more."

"I am Crystal?"

"Of course."

"How can you be so sure?"

"Because you can make a difference. There's a new dark lord." Said the Legendary Hero.

"A dark lord?"

"Yes."

"What's his name?"

"Malcolm."

"Malcolm?"

"Yes."

"I want to keep my power," Krell said.

"You shall."

"Without my power, I'm nothing."

"You like seeing Belinda. Right?"

"I do."

"Would you marry her?"

"I think I would."

"But, how can you turn her to being good?"

"By giving her a choice."

"Oh. That's interesting."

"It is Krell. So, this is your choice. To live here in Ashello forever and not see Belinda or live with Rone and Crystal in my dimension where I  live."

"You serious Legendary Hero?"

"I'm serious." And for the record my real name is Demetrius. "So, what's your choice, Krell?

Rone and Crystal? Would you be ok with me living with you?"

"There's only one concern I have, Krell."

"And what would that be Crystal?"

"That you're not evil anymore."

"I've been evil all my life. Is there any way that I can be good? Can you forgive me for the things I have done?"

"Of course I can, Krell."

"What would Belinda do if she saw me being good? Would she hurt me?"

"She probably would try, but I won't let that happen."

 "Ok. Demetrius . I'll come with you."

"Krell, there's one last thing you need to know."

"What's that?"

"I have a lot of people who have powers that could hurt you. But, I'll make sure that they don't."

"Thank you, Demetrius."

"You're welcome. Let's go back to my home.

Are you ready to get Nicholas and David?"

"Yes."

"Krell, do you want to come with me?"

"Ok."

 "Hey, everybody. I'm back," Demetrius said.

"Hey Demetrius."

Pointing at Krell, "who's this person, Demetrius?" Max said.

"His name is Krell. He's a sorcerer."

"Sorcerer?"

Max spoke up. "I'll take him on."

"Max! Don't hurt him."

"Why not?"

"He may be a sorcerer, but he's trying to be a good person. Cut him some slack."

"I'm sorry." Max reached out. "I'm Max. Nice to meet you, Krell."

So what's the plan, said Claire.

I'm training you, the legendary Hero said.

Who will rescue Eric? Said summer.

In addition to Crystal and Rone it will be Spider-Man David and Nicholas.

That's a great lineup, said Mary.

It is. Let's get Nicholas and David.

# Chapter 13 Nicholas and David

Nicholas and David were in Brackinova roaming around.

Well it looks like we made it safely, said Krell

Rone and Crystal nodded in assent. Let's try and find Nicholas and David.

Perhaps we can ask these guards. Said Krell.

Halt!! State your business!!

We are looking for Nicholas and David. Have you seen them?

Well yes. We have.

That's interesting Nicholas.

What?

I see two people talking to the guards. Are they friend? Or foe.

We're about to find out.

They ran to where the guards were.

Ah!! There they are. Said Crystal

Rone! Crystal! What a surprise!!

What brings you here to Brackinova? Said Nicholas

Well. We have some bad news. Said Rone.

Has Eric turned evil again?

No. Worse. He's been captured by Belinda. Said Crystal.

That's not good David.

It surely isn't. We should rescue him. But where can we go?

Well you're not going to like it, said Crystal. The villains lair. We can't do it alone.

So that means we're coming with you?

You're right David. Said Rone.

Let's go then. The sooner the better. Said David.

We brought you wands so you can follow us.

Ok. Let's go, said Nicholas.

They were transported to the villain's lair.

# Chapter 14
## Infiltrating the Lair

They made it safely to the lair. They talked in low voices.

Do you see that wall of vines? We can't go through there. Said Crystal. So what should we do?

Hmm… I think that we should make a diversion said David.

A diversion?

Yeah. Like causing a distraction.

It seems clear that I should enter while you're having the diversion. Nicholas said. That way I can slip in and find where Eric is.

Not a bad idea, Nicholas, said Rone. What about Daisy though? She's a sorceress.

That's a good point, said Crystal. We both are sorceresses so I could trick her and lock her in a closet or something.

Suddenly Spider-Man appeared on the wall.

Yes. He said in a quiet tone. I like your plan.

Spider-Man? What are you doing here?

Here to rescue Eric of course.

I can cause the diversion. I'm Spider-Man.

So what do you intend to do?

What I will do is scour the area and find where Eric is. In fact I know where Eric is.

You do? Where?

3rd floor. With Belinda.

I knew it. Said Crystal. How are we going to get up there with all the guards?

You leave that to me! Spidey said.

I'll start on the first floor and once Belinda is called down on the first floor you Crystal will tie up Daisy.

As for you Nicholas and David, you David will cause a diversion on the second floor.

Nicholas. You will conceal yourself on the third floor.

And you Crystal. After you tie up Daisy, have Belinda follow you to the third floor and we'll convince her to let Eric go.

What about me?

You Krell? Stay on the third floor and block the villains from accessing it. If we do this correctly we will successfully rescue Eric without being captured ourselves.

We have a plan. Be careful Spider-Man!

I give you my word!

Everyone did their job and found Eric!

# Chapter 15
## Belinda and Krell Reunite

Eric shouted, "Let me Out!"

"You're not going anywhere."

"We're back," Nicholas David Rone and Crystal exclaimed.

"Why are you here?"

"We want to see Eric."

"You can't rescue Eric."

"That's not our intention."

"It isn't? Nope."

"We have someone here to see you."

"Who is it?

"Take a look."

Krell! What are you doing here? ``I thought you were wreaking havoc in Ashello."

"I was. But, I've changed."

"Changed? How?"

"The Legendary Hero gave me a choice. I could stay in Ashello or be with you. The thing is. I love you. Do you love me?"

"Of course. Can you let Eric out Belinda?'

"I'm not sure. I truly enjoy having Eric in my hands as my captive and so has everyone else. Besides, I love having him.

You have a choice. You either can stay with me or you will stay captive with the legendary hero.

Belinda looked at Eric. She looked at Krell.

Eric looked at her with pleading eyes.

We really have had fun together. Haven't we Eric.

Eric nodded. Belinda untied Eric and removed the handkerchief from his mouth.

I've heard everything that has been said.

I remember that we had a good bond. We were close, Belinda.

Yes. We were Eric.

I'm glad you're all here to rescue me.

Belinda's tears came down her cheek.

I'm sorry Eric.

I forgive you Belinda. And I'm happy that you're letting me go. So let me get this straight. Krell?

Yes Eric?

You want to marry Belinda. Isn't that right?

Yes.

Eric?

Yes Nicholas?

I hear villains are coming this way!! We need to get out of here before we're spotted.

Eric said quietly and quickly, Hold my hands!

They held hands.

He said with distinction, PORIFAY. Take us to Eric's Domain.

They were all transported.


I thought I heard something, said the vine villain.

Let's check it out.

They looked in Belinda's room. It was empty.

Oh my gosh!! Malcolm is going to be furious.

After all his hard work Eric escaped. But what happened with Belinda? Was she captured?

Malcolm was patrolling the villains' lair. He had an evil smile on his face.

So how is our prisoner Eric doing?

Uh. That seems to be the problem.

What problem? You don't mean to say that he escaped do you?

The villains looked on in fear.

Malcolm's fiery red eyes flashed with anger.

HE ESCAPED!!!???!!  How!!!!???!

Somehow the four heroes rescued him. They created quite a diversion that we didn't even see one  of them. But we saw two swordsmen and a sorceress.

Where was Daisy when they arrived?

We didn't see Daisy. Somehow they outsmarted us and tied her up in one of the rooms.

Don't you realize that this is the best lair where heroes can easily get captured?

We know it all too well.

There's no way they could've gotten in without help from the outside. Who else could've it been?

I know only one hero who has a talent for disruption as well as crawling on walls.  SPIDER-MAN!!

# The Return of Braille

We made it!! It feels so good to be back in my domain, said Eric. Thanks for rescuing me.

It was our pleasure Eric!

I was the one who orchestrated the plan!

Thank you Spider-Man!! I don't know what I would've done without you.

You couldn't have done it without them!! And you all did very very well! Said Braille with a smile.

Eric couldn't believe his eyes.

Braille!! You're back!! I knew you would come!!

I told you I'd be back. You just needed to wait a little bit longer.

Malcolm hasn't been defeated yet Eric!

I know Belinda! He will be. I have a feeling he's having a rampage right now at the villain's lair.

In your state he would try to force you to capture me again but I won't let that happen.

And what about my oldest brother Braze?

Braze? I will confront him very soon. But first I must stop your older brother.

He's too powerful Eric!

I'm powerful too! In fact, Demetrius has given me all of his powers.

He has?

You can trust me!

Well said Eric!! Said Braille. I think you're ready.

Not quite.

What else could be missing?

Well Braille I think it's a good time for all of us to sleep now. We have a lot to prepare for tomorrow.

Yes. We do. One last thing before we go to bed. I'm proud of all of you. You've really done well.

*Everyone hugged each other and went to sleep.*

*You've made me so angry, Spider-Man !! Said Malcolm. I will get my sister back for what you've done and you will pay. Somehow, someway. You're going to pay.*

## Preparations for Battle

Braille was inside the lab thinking.

It seems that Malcolm is still at large and Belinda and Krell are good now. I can't change the settings on the computer. If I do, Braze will find me again. I think it's important for me to call Malcolm and meet at the battlefield here in Eric's Domain. It is here where I've seen everything being damaged. It is here where this fun stuff ends. Computer?

Yes?

Call Villains lair.

That's dangerous!! Are you sure?

Yes!!

Ok. Calling now.

*Malcolm was storming around when one of the villains called for him.*

What?? Can't you see I'm angry? I want to be alone!

But Malcolm. There's a phone call.

Phone call? Give it to me. Please!

This is Malcolm! What do you want?

You know who I am. And your older brother has tried to capture me many times.

I know who you are! Braille!! What till my brother hears about this.

Hear me out Malcolm!! Your brother wants me and I want him. How about we meet. Face To Face! Where **you** damaged everything in Eric's Domain. You've caused too much damage here and you will pay.

Is that a threat? Fine! I'll come over and bring my friends with me.

Spider-Man didn't capture Belinda. He just got Krell to change Belinda into a good person.

Oh! That actually makes me feel better. So she wasn't captured? Correct.

I'll do as you ask Braille!

One last thing! **Don't call your brother!!** I'll call him myself.

It's a deal then. See you soon.

*Malcolm felt relieved about Belinda.*

It's time my friends!

Time for what? Said vine villain.

It's time for the great battle.

Let's capture those heroes!

*Eric's Domain. Here we Come!!*


*Meanwhile in Eric's Domain.....*


Braille got out of the shed. Everyone was outside.

Braille!! What's going on? Said Demetrius.

I just talked with Malcolm.

You talked to Malcolm?! Why?

Because he's done enough damage. He's on his way.

We're going to stop him. Eric?

Yes?

You've trained the family of powers well?

I have.

Are you ready everyone?

Yes. We are.

Are you prepared to face your brother Belinda?

I am.

What about you Krell? Are you ready?

I am. Max and I should be able to stop him.

*Meanwhile, Back at the princesses castle*

Aren't you girls ready to go to Eric's Domain yet? Said the queen.

We are!!

Wait a minute!! Said the king

Yes dear?

It's not safe!!

Why not? Said Isabelle.

Because the great battle is about to happen.

Are you sure?

Yes. I'll let you know when it's safe.

…………………

It's time to stop Malcolm! Said Eric.

I hear them coming. Said Demetrius.

Get ready to fight!! We fight on the battlefield.

*Everyone waited in anticipation as they waited in the field.*

# Chapter
# The Final Battle


*Eric, Krell, Belinda, and everyone else waited patiently in the field.*

Ah!! We have arrived. Said Malcolm. Where is everyone?
Looking for us Malcolm? Here we are! Said Eric.
Malcolm sneered. It's the famous Eric Thompson. The superhero.
Villains!! Attack!!
Claire went invisible. Matt started punching, Max and Krell faced
Malcolm. Belinda and Crystal faced Daisy. Rone and David fought with
their swords. Braille disappeared into the trees. Nicholas kept his
distance and fired arrows as well as Linda. Ben fought as a ninja. Dash
sped around and knocked villains down right and left.
Now you see what kind of army I have Malcolm! Said Eric. Surrender
and we will let you walk away unharmed. If you don't I will send you
away. Your brother will be next.
Malcolm faced Eric and said with an evil smile, you have no idea what
my brother is capable of. He was the one who's almost captured Braille
multiple times. You don't stand a chance against him! How quaint! Two
sorcerers against me! You can't stop me! I've had lots of experience. Not
even you Eric can stop me!
You have no idea what I'm capable of, Malcolm!
STRASINKO!!
A regular spell!! You're going to have to do better than **THAT** as he
brushed it aside.
Max!! Krell!! Pin him down!! I'm going to increase my power!
Max threw everything he had at him. Malcolm was able to shield himself
somehow.
Keep up the pressure Max!! Said Krell

I'm going to try something.

He tightened his fist which started to power up. He punched with full power. The shield broke!

Noooooo!!!! Said Malcolm.

I got you now Malcolm! Said Max.

He put him on the wall.

NOW Eric!!

Eric's power was so strong. It was glowing. Even Belinda saw it.

Everyone saw Eric glowing.

***NOW ERIC!!***

Eric went right up to Malcolm!

**BLAST!!**

Malcolm went soaring through the sky.

He was never heard of or seen again.

Retreat!! Said the villains.

*Brother! Said Braze. I will stop Eric for what he's done.*

*It is time! My daughters. Said the king.*

# Chapter
# The Wedding

*Eric and everybody went back to Eric Thompson's domain.*

Well done Eric!! You did very well.

Thank you Braille. I'm glad you're here.

Me too. I've never glowed like you did. How did you do that Eric?

Demetrius gave me his powers. So I not only can cast spells. I can become anything.

Belinda said to Daisy, stay with us!!

I don't know if I can. I'm still evil!

I can fix that. Said Eric.

Daisy. Look at me. You remember what it was like for us to be evil together?

I do.

We had a good bond that you even did what Belinda asked you to do.

That's right.

You have a choice. You can be captive, or you can stay with us and last forever. You can be a sorceress and become a guardian. What do you think of that?

She paused. I think it's a good idea. I understand.

You've made a good decision. By the way, Krell and Belinda are going to get married.

Really?

Yes.

So you both want to marry each other? Said Braille

We do.

Then I will conduct your ceremony.

Are you ready to exchange your vows?

Vows?

It's a life commitment. You basically say how you feel.

We understand now. Thanks.

You're first Krell.

Thanks Braille.

I, Krell solemnly honor your wishes and be your partner. I promise to keep you safe and love you till the day I die.

I, Belinda, promise to use my powers wisely as well as being honest with you and live until my last dying breath.

Do you Krell take Belinda to be your lawfully wedded wife to love, honor, and cherish, till death do you part?"

Krell said, "I do."

Do you Belinda take Krell to be your lawfully wedded husband to love, honor, and cherish, till death do you part?'

Belinda said, "I do."

"If anyone thinks that these two should not be married. Speak now, for forever hold your peace… By the power vested in me, I now pronounce you man and wife. You may kiss the bride."

*Everyone else individually did their ceremonies.*

"This is awesome." Everyone shouted with joy.

Eric said, "I'm amazed that all of you have chosen to be married. You have made a great decision. I welcome you into the circle of trust with the legendary hero."

Eric waved a hearty goodbye. "Farewell, Demetrius."

*Epilogue*

Eric stood proudly amongst his friends. "Thank you all for everything. If it wasn't for you Max and Krell I wouldn't have stopped Malcolm. He was more powerful than I was. But together we stopped him. And thank you for stepping into the light to be on my side. Well done everybody. I will miss you all. I am so happy I trained you. You were ready. Farewell everyone. I hope to see you all again someday. Belinda and Krell, wherever you go, there will be evil or good. Please always choose the good. I hope that you both live a happy life."

"We will, Eric. Thank you. If it wasn't for you we never would've stopped Malcolm's army. Farewell my friends." Braille?

Yes Eric?

Will you tell me what happened to your father someday?

I will. There is something else I want you to help with.

And what's that?

To train my son and daughter.

I will. But first I should find someone. Someone who you said I should train. Sam!

Oh yeah!! I almost forgot about him. Thanks for reminding me Eric.

Will I ever see you again?

You will. Once you've trained Sam my boy and girl
will be of age for you to train.
Thanks again. For everything Braille.
It was my pleasure.
Farewell! Until we meet again.

*Eric Thompson, the hero, left Eric's domain and
went home. The family went their separate ways.
Belinda and Krell lived happily ever after.*

The End.

# About the Author

My name is Eric Kelly Thompson and I am a young man with autism. I am a Special Olympics athlete. I have been part of the smart reading program where I learned the importance of reading books. My reading efforts and my personal journey with autism gave me the desire to write this very special book.

I hope this book will help you understand what autism is and how to respect those with disabilities.

I was athlete of the year for 2010. This is where you can find the link where I spoke:

https://www.youtube.com/watch?v=k4snA6bw0Zc&feature=youtube

Here's a quick look for my next book:

# Sam's Destiny

# Introduction

In the first book of the Legendary Hero Series, two warriors, whose names were Elphias and Frederick of Galvestein were trained by the Legendary Hero. They helped three princesses rescue their oldest sister from the evil witch Belinda. In the battle against Belinda, Eric (the author) had help from a swordsman named Rone and a Sorceress named Crystal. Belinda had help from an evil Sorceress named Daisy and a sorcerer named Krell. Her brother Malcolm also joined in on her side. Eric trained a family with superpowers who helped rescue Eric and others. Belinda and Krell were married, but unbeknownst to Eric and the Legendary Hero There's another evil sorcerer, Braze, and his sister Maribel and another sorceress named Veronica. Their current plan is to capture the Legendary Hero.

Made in the USA
Monee, IL
24 May 2022

96481358R10114